SEVEN DAYS AFTER

MARKUS CHAMBERS

IMMERSIVE BOOKS

ISBN: 979-8-98-707990-4 (US trade), 979-8-98-707991-1 (ebook)

Printed in the United States of America

Content Warning

This story includes elements that might not be suitable for some readers. Themes such as sexual assault and suicide are mentioned. There are other themes that some may find triggering. Readers who may be sensitive to these elements, please take note.

To the ones who said I couldn't, and for the ones who said I could

1

THE BEGINNING OF THE END

"I know not with what weapons World War III will be fought, but World War IV will be fought with sticks and stones."

ALBERT EINSTEIN

Miles Winstead burst through the locker room door and dropped to his knees before the nearest commode. He heaved and heaved, but nothing came out. Gripping the cool, wet porcelain—*please let that liquid be condensation*—he took a deep breath, the stink of the toilet water making him heave some more. But still, nothing. The gigantic ball of anxiety rolled around in the pit of his stomach. The sensation was so familiar to him that he might have come to think of it as an old friend by now if it didn't feel so much like death.

Get it together, Miles. You can do this. It's just a speech. Taking another deep breath, he stood and left the stall. He ventured back into the changing area and started pacing. Back and forth he went, past the coach's den and rows of lockers, until his stomach and mind finally began to quiet.

After a minute more, he finally stopped and gathered his

composure. Leaning against the white-painted cinderblock wall, he sank his hands in the pockets of his dress slacks and fished out an index card. It had a few single words written on it: *experience, college, friendships, sports*, all surrounding the word *life*. The crude diagram was meant to guide him through the Valedictorian speech he'd been rehearsing for the past week should his memory fail him. Yet when he looked down at the card, the words were meaningless. Disconnected.

Okay, worst case, I just read the damn thing. Miles reminded himself that a copy of the full speech, complete with the principal's required seal of approval on the first page, was already on the podium on stage. He had insisted on placing it there himself.

But would that be the worst case, really? he wondered, his mind moving on to ever more disastrous scenarios. What if he chokes? Stutters? Makes a complete ass of himself in front of everyone? He shuddered as he pictured it: all his classmates and their parents laughing and pointing at him as he trips on the stage and crashes into the podium. Maybe he'd knock his front teeth out. Get a concussion.

Miles shook his head vigorously to try to rid himself of his negative thoughts. He didn't want his classmates' last impression of him to be awash in nervousness, awkwardness, and failure. He looked in the mirror and tried to exhale all his fears the way he learned from an internet video. He added an affirmation for good measure.

I can do this.

Miles examined his reflection, trying his best to ignore

the stress bags under his eyes and bubbling acne behind his chin stubble. He removed his cap, whisked his hands through his dirty-blond hair to throw it to the side, then returned the cap to his head.

Miles was just about to march out the door when he heard voices in the corridor outside the locker room. Unsure of who the voices belonged to, he jumped back and glued himself to the wall to hide.

He listened closely as the steel door flew open. "Five bucks says he'll be too chicken shit to even get up on the stage," a male voice said.

"Ten bucks says he gets up there and pukes," said another. The two laughed and the sound of hands slapping in a high five followed.

Miles knew exactly who the voices belonged to. He held his breath and clung to the cement of the cinderblock wall like a chameleon hiding from its prey. *Maybe they'll just leave. Maybe they'll just . . .*

"Well, well, well," Eddie's sneer put an end to that wishful thinking. "Speak of the devil."

"What do you guys want?" Miles asked, embarrassed at the squeak in his voice.

"I dunno." Eddie sniffled. "How 'bout we kick your ass one last time? As a farewell gift."

"Yeah," Rick added. "Something to remember us by." He cracked his knuckles together.

"It's been four years guys. Give it a rest already," Miles said, inching toward the door.

Eddie pressed his hand against the wall, preventing Miles from going any further. "What's the rush?"

Miles took a step back to get out from under Eddie's towering frame. As he did, one of the overhead lights bounced off a fish hook stuck on the brim of Eddie's camouflaged baseball cap, and Miles wondered if it was intended for him. "No rush. Just wanna graduate and get out of here. Just like you guys."

"You ain't nothin' like us, ass wipe," Rick said. He emphasized his point by spitting a wad of spent chewing tobacco against the white wall over Miles's head.

By this time, Miles felt the sweat trickling down his sides, coating his ribs in a gloss of fear and shame as he quaked in his wingtips. The sweat soaked his dress shirt and darkened his pine-green gown. As Eddie and Rick inched closer, their unshaven faces glaring down at him, Miles's breathing deepened. He saw exactly two choices: Make a run for it like a wimp, or stand up to these guys and be the man he so desperately wanted to be. The cool kid. Someone everyone could respect. Someone strong.

No more running.

Miles made his decision. As Eddie geared up for the gut punch of the century, Miles kneed him right in the balls and elbowed Rick in the chest, shoving them both out of the way and making a dash for the door. He made it one proud, glorious step before Rick managed to snatch up the tail of his gown and pull him into a chokehold.

"That's a real cheap shot, Miles," Eddie murmured, grabbing at his crotch in pain.

"What are you waiting for? Hit him!" Rick said, wedging himself between the wall and locker to get a better hold on Miles.

Miles shook profusely, trying to escape Rick's grasp, but to no avail. Eddie regained his stance, inhaled deeply, and landed a vicious blow to Miles's stomach. Miles groaned, wanting to hunch over and die, but couldn't because of Rick's hold on him. Eddie hit him again, his knuckles crunching upon impact against Miles's ribcage. And then he aimed for Miles's jaw. Third times the charm. The last blow likely would've knocked Miles out, but at the last second Miles moved, and the punch caught him in the cheek instead, knocking his glasses from his face. They landed on the mud-tiled floor.

"My turn!" Rick yelled, releasing Miles and pushing him against the wall. Miles slid to the floor and curled into the fetal position, his head tucked like a turtle, arms cradling his aching stomach.

Rick hadn't gotten but one kick in when the door to the locker room burst open. Coach Windsor had caught two of his top football players in the act of beating a fellow student to a pulp. He ripped the boys off Miles and threw them against a set of lockers, both of them cracking their shoulders against the cold metal.

"What the hell!" Rick yelled, rubbing his shoulder. "You can't do that to us."

"Shut it," the coach shot back. "Just like you can't do what you two were just doing to him, right?" He looked over at Miles on the floor. "You okay?" He handed him his glasses.

Miles peered up at the coach, taking in his broad shoulders, thick hairy forearms, and unbelievably short board-shorts. He never thought he'd be so happy to see this beast of a man. "Been better, but I'm good."

"Good," Coach Windsor said. Then to Eddie and Rick, he added: "You two, go to the main office and wait until I get there. And don't you go disappearing, or I'll make sure you don't graduate 'til you're 25."

Coach Windsor reached for Miles to help him up as Rick and Eddie made their exits. Then he glanced at his watch and sighed. "They're going to be waiting for at least an hour. Rats."

They sat on the locker room bench, Miles licking the blood from his swollen lip.

"Did you at least try to fight back?" Coach Windsor asked. "Because there's not always going to be someone around to save you." He stood and grabbed a few pieces of toilet paper from the nearest stall and handed them to Miles.

Miles pressed them against the tiny cut on his lip to stop the bleeding, then patted it dry. "This time I did. And it felt good, even though I still lost."

"At least you tried." Coach Windsor said, patting Miles on the shoulder.

They shared a moment of silence until the rustling of footsteps on gymnasium bleachers and music blaring from the PA system wafted into the locker room from overhead.

"You still want to do your speech?" Coach Windsor asked. "Because you don't have to if you don't want to. I can talk to—"

"Thanks, but I do. I need to." Miles was done with excuses. He wasn't crazy about the idea of walking up on that stage in front of all his classmates looking the way he did at that moment--defeated and beat down--but something inside him said to do it. "I don't know why, but I do."

Coach Windsor stood, patting Miles on the back. "Then you better get up there. I'll be right behind you after I take a piss." He walked to one of the urinals and was too busy unbuttoning his fly to notice as Miles thrust his chin into the air, puffed up his chest, and marched out of the locker room, the picture of confidence.

———

YOU'VE GOT THIS.

Miles collected himself, carefully slowing his breathing as he approached the front of the gymnasium.

I hope they don't laugh.

He gingerly climbed the creaky steps of the portable metal stage, then, being careful not to trip and fall, walked to the faux-wood podium that stood in front of the crowd.

As soon as he rested his hands on the varnished wood surface, he froze—still like a corpse, staring out at the warm, blinding lights reflecting off the freshly waxed floors, the green banners marking Redmond High's greatest accomplishments hanging from the ceiling, and the five hundred people who were surely waiting for him to make a fool of himself.

"Get on with it!" some kid shouted from the stands. Laughter rippled through the gathered mass, but Miles didn't move. His heart pounded, increasing in intensity by the second, almost exploding out of his chest like a grenade.

Just breathe.

He let the deep breath fill him, at once drawing him up to the ceiling and down through the floor. He searched the room for his parents but instead found his girlfriend, Alice Winters, beaming at him, and a calmness instantly fell over him. He smiled back, nudged his glasses up onto the bridge of his nose, then reached for the index card in his pocket.

Miles leaned into the microphone and looked down at the crowd before him. Some were still tittering over his failure to speak, others were shifting in their seats, but none, as far as he could tell, looked particularly eager to hear about Miles Winstead's thoughts on life's great mysteries. And that was fine, Miles realized suddenly because that wasn't what he wanted to share with them at that moment.

Relaxing his shoulders, Miles crumpled up his index card and tossed it over his shoulder, causing the room to fall silent.

Go big or go home.

"I'm not gonna bore you guys with the generic inspirational speech. How about I give you something real instead?"

Miles noted the principal's puzzled look and hoped she

wouldn't pull the plug on the microphone before he got the chance to get everything he had to say off his chest.

"Life is terrible," Miles began. "Life is hard. And I'm not just talking about school either. *Yeah,* you get one or two great experiences, but for the most part, the rest of life is boring and uneventful. Your existence is pretty much determined by who your parents are and how much money they make. It sounds depressing, right? Whether you're cool, whether you're attractive, whether you're popular, none of that matters once you walk out that door. If you actually bothered to learn anything while you were here, you've got a chance." Miles wiped the drops of sweat from his forehead and continued. "Just focus on your education, and you'll show up at reunion making twice the amount of money as the good-looking meatheads sitting around you right now. At least that's what they say. As for the rest of you"—his mouth was so close to the mic by now his lips could almost brush it —"you can all go fuck—"

That was as far as he got in his contemporaneous speech before the microphone went dead. He'd been cut off by the staff sound engineer.

A cold mic couldn't stop Miles.

"You can all go fuck yourselves! Each and every one of you!" Miles continued, shouting while throwing up both middle fingers and flinging them around at the crowd.

The crowd sat motionless, stunned; some faces grew red with fury while others grew red with embarrassment. Amid the silence, the principal grabbed Miles by the arm and started pulling him off the stage.

A clap rang out from the bleachers. Then another. Miles turned toward the crowd and once again spotted Alice, only this time she was standing and applauding, with a look of pride on her face. Soon, the rest of his classmates joined in, clapping, cheering, and stomping their feet. Miles Winstead, of all people, had turned their boring graduation ceremony into an event they would never forget.

White smoke belched from under the grill's lid as Miles's father, Rodger, opened it to flip the burgers and dogs. He placed the last of the burgers on a Pyrex plate, then set the plate down on the side table next to the potato salad, baked beans, and chips.

"That was a *terrible* speech," he said to his son when Miles returned for seconds. "I expected more from you. Something *appropriate* at least."

Ignoring his father's comment, Miles dropped another burger onto his plate and went for the spoon in the potato salad.

"I know you hear me." He tugged at Miles's shoulder, stopping him from further preparing his second plate. "You're lucky the principal didn't hold you back for that stunt you pulled. What do you have to say for yourself?"

Miles picked up the ketchup bottle and squeezed it, sending a mountain of thick red sauce atop his beef patty.

"Well, I could ask you the same thing." He hoped his father could sense the unhappiness in the tone of his voice.

Rodger placed the tongs and spatula on the table next to the grill and rested his hand on Miles's shoulder. "If this is about the bike, I'm sorry. You know we couldn't afford much this year. But I *promise* we'll get it for you next year. Okay?"

"Whatever." Miles rolled his eyes before storming off, venturing back through the maze of distant relatives and returning to his spot on the wrought-iron bench in the corner of the backyard. He knew why his parents couldn't afford his graduation gift. He just didn't want to cut them any slack.

"Hey bucko," Uncle Cliff said, joining him on the bench. "I'm so proud of you. Believe your parents are, too."

Miles wiped his mouth with a napkin. "Doesn't seem like it. They didn't even get me a gift!"

"Oh, they didn't now?" Cliff chuckled, looking around the backyard at all the family members that had come to show support; Miles's many cousins, young and old, throwing around the Frisbee, his aunt talking shop with the neighbors, and his other uncle refilling the cooler with a fresh bag of ice. All of them were dressed in the same matching dark-green shirts that represented the schools' colors.

"Well, you know a lot has happened this year." He turned to Miles. "With your father getting laid off and all, money's a little tight right now. Things'll get better."

Miles's facial expression indicated he didn't care about his parents' problems one bit.

"I shouldn't tell you this, but your grandfather had no life insurance. So when he passed, they had to come out of pocket to cover his funeral expenses. And that stuff ain't cheap. I'll admit I only chipped in a little, your uncle Pete did, too, from what we could spare, but the majority of it fell on your parents." Cliff inhaled deeply. "So if anything you might want to cut him some slack. Remember, he's working a job now, but it still doesn't match what he used to make."

Maybe I was hard on Dad.

Miles sank his head. He had made a fool of himself. Being pissed at a couple of high school bullies didn't give him an excuse to be an asshole to his father.

Before he could even think any further into his self-flagellation, Cliff asked, "Were you hoping for something in particular?"

"A motorcycle. I took the class and everything. Paid for it with the money I saved up from the job I had last summer."

A Frisbee floated toward them, landing in Cliff's lap. One of Miles's cousins ran up and held out his hand, waiting for Cliff to return the throw. "You gonna play with us, Miles?"

Miles thought about it for a second. "Maybe later. I'm still eating."

Cliff threw it back to little Charlie, then watched him return to the middle of the yard and toss it to another cousin. "Can you believe it? We can't even get half these people together for Thanksgiving dinner."

"So what, graduating high school is a bigger deal than

major holidays around here?" Miles joked, his mouth full of potato salad.

Cliff turned to him with a serious look. "Yes, Miles, I think it is. Some of us *older* folk didn't graduate, you know. And the ones that did, didn't further their education. It's kind of a big deal for the younger generation to be betterin' yourselves. I for one am very proud of you for wanting to go to college. And scoring a full ride to the university! That's just unheard of in this family." He patted Miles on the thigh. "Well, I'm going to grab another plate before it's too late." Standing from the bench, he turned and added: "Don't be a stranger now, okay?"

Miles smiled. "I won't."

As Cliff walked off to grab another plate, Miles heard a familiar voice rising over the muffled sea of shit-talking and corny jokes being exchanged between his father and uncles. He turned toward the pleasant sound and found Alice entering through the back gate in their white picket fence.

Alice had shunned the school spirit dress code and worn Miles's favorite dress instead, and he appreciated the decision as she walked toward him. She looked beautiful. The baby-blue dress caused her radiant skin and emerald-green eyes to glisten in the sun. A slight breeze of wind followed her into the backyard, whirling her shoulder-length, auburn hair around her face and revealing those seasonal freckles on her cheeks he adored so much.

I am the luckiest guy on earth.

"Did you save me any food?" Alice joked.

She held out her hand. Chuckling, Miles grabbed it. She

pulled him up off the bench, wrapped him in a bear hug, and kissed him on the lips.

Staring deep into her eyes, Miles said, "You know, getting into a relationship with you was the best thing that ever happened to me. Really, the only monumental moment in my life."

She beamed. "I could say the same."

Miles and Alice had been together for two years, and Miles considered them the best years of his life, despite everything else he had endured in high school. He'd do it all again as long as he still had Alice by his side.

"I'm so proud of you," she said. "And that speech, Miles..." She drew in a breath. "It didn't even sound like you!"

Miles blushed at her enthusiasm. "It's the *new* me."

Alice *mhmm'd* at his reply with a skeptical smile. "How about we go for a walk then? *Mr. It's-the-New-Me.*"

"But what about the party?" he asked.

Though he didn't really want to be there, surrounded by family members he hadn't seen since he was a child, Miles assumed being present for a gathering celebrating himself was the right thing to do.

"I don't think they'll mind." Alice turned, smiled, and waved kindly at Elaine and Rodger from a distance. Over the course of her relationship with Miles, Alice had practically become a member of the Winstead family: coming over almost every day after school to do homework and joining in family activities whenever they'd arise. She turned back to

Miles. "There's, like, a hundred people here. They probably won't even notice we've gone."

Alice and Miles strolled out of the backyard, leaving the fence to close with a heavy thud.

"You're okay with your son leaving the party?" Cliff asked Rodger, pointing at the closed gate.

Rodger scoffed. "No. But he's not the type to stray too far from the nest if you catch my drift. They're probably going to walk around the block, then come right back. That's all. I bet they won't even be gone ten minutes."

———

MILES KICKED at a rock on the gravel path down near the murky lake two blocks from his house as Alice walked beside him. With every step they took the earth crunched beneath their feet. As the sun began to set, the temperature fell, and what was once a pleasant breeze quickly turned bitter and cold. Miles tucked his hands into the pockets of his jeans, and Alice tightened the top button on her dress.

"I'm so glad this chapter of my life is over." Miles exhaled a sigh of relief. "Now I can finally be happy... finally live."

"I've heard you go on and on about not being happy for the past six months now. Quite frankly I'm sick of it," Alice blurted out.

"Wait, what!" Miles exclaimed, stopping to turn around. "Why are *you* sick of it?

"Because it sounds like you're gonna kill yourself! And I

don't wanna lose you." Alice reached for his face, brushing her thumb against his cheek. "Why aren't you happy? 'Cause the way I see it, you've got it made."

"Well, I don't."

"What do you mean, you don't?"

"I just don't alright?" Miles shot back, his tone sharp.

Alice reached for his hand, but he yanked it away. "Miles, your family loves you. I love you. You might be a little anxious and corny, but that's just who you are. And I like who you are."

"Well, who I am sucks!" He marched down the trail, Alice chasing after him.

"Miles, you don't suck. You might be a little overly anxious, but I like that about you." Grabbing his arm, she spun him around. "I remember it like it was yesterday; when we first met, you were too scared to even talk to me on the bus." She giggled. "But then you ended up having to show me around campus. I'll never forget it. You stuttered almost every other word." She grabbed his hand. "And now look, you don't even stutter anymore. Not one bit. See, you've changed so much already without even realizing it."

"That's not what I'm talking about, Alice." Miles broke from her grasp and climbed a few nearby rocks and took comfort on a boulder, his ass cushioned by the thick moss that had accumulated over years of growth.

She joined him.

"Then what?" Alice asked, concerned for his well-being. "What *are you* talking about? If it's not about changing for the better or being happy, then what is it?"

Miles didn't want to burden Alice with his troubles, knowing she had her own to deal with, but he couldn't hold it in anymore. He also knew she'd keep asking if he didn't speak his truth. So it was time to come out with it.

"It's not that I'm not happy, Alice. I just don't wanna spend my entire life being a nobody."

"Miles, you're not a nobody."

"Yes, I am! People walked all over me at school. My parents even do it sometimes, guilting me into doing things I don't even wanna do."

"Like what?" she asked.

"Well, to be honest, I didn't even wanna go to college. My parents just want me to. I have no clue what I wanna do with my life. And I don't wanna just pick something only to realize when I'm their age that I never really lived 'cause I was so busy working." Jumping up from the rock and standing tall, Miles scoffed. "I wanna experience things, you know? Like how superheroes and spies do in the movies. I wanna be a somebody."

Hearing a rustling in the leaves, he stopped talking. He looked to his left and spotted a doe running off, losing sight of it in the brush.

"I wanna travel the world," he continued. "Ride a motorcycle. Hike Kilimanjaro. Live a life full of excitement! Don't you?"

"I do. But Miles, you do know a majority of that stuff's fake, right? Most people just use their vacation time once or twice a year to do such things."

Miles turned to Alice. "Well, I wanna do it all year. And I want you by my side when I do it."

"Well, I'd love to be there by your side, but there's one problem. Money."

"No, there's two," Miles shot back.

"Two?" Alice questioned as if she had misheard.

"Yes. My anxiety." He turned away in shame. "Even with the pills—they don't help much. To tell you the truth, I sweat through my entire shirt this morning before *and* during my speech. I was soaked afterward, that's why I changed." He motioned to his blue jeans and green polo. "If it weren't for you and those pills giving me confidence—*and maybe that unexpected shot of post-beatdown adrenaline*—I don't think I could've said what I said on that stage today."

Alice slowly reached for his hand, turning him toward her and sitting him back down on the rock. "Everybody has stage fright, Miles. It's normal. Knowing who you are and seeing you *actually* finish a speech says a lot. You're just overthinking things. Relax. You're moving at just the right pace."

Seeing the judgment-free smile planted on Alice's face gave Miles a sense of reassurance. The twinkle in her eyes was just an added plus.

He beamed. "I guess you're right. I just need to relax. Come this time next year, once you graduate, we'll both be off on our own, traveling to God knows where to experience it all! With no anxiety to hold me back."

"Only the money to do it with, right?" Alice joked with a grin. "Now, are you ready for your gift?"

"Sure."

Alice reached for Miles's crotch, unzipping his jeans.

Miles pushed her hand away. "Hey! We can't do that out here."

"Why not? It's not like someone's watching." She went in again. "You wanted to live a life full of excitement, right?"

Miles nodded.

"Okay then. Let's start with a simple hand job."

3

The grandfather clock in the hall struck eight while Miles carried the trash through the kitchen where his mother, Elaine, finished up the last few dishes. Trash pickup was first thing Monday morning, and since it was officially summer, Miles didn't want to have to wake up early to put the bins out before the trucks arrived. Rodger flipped through channels on the television in the living room as Miles headed for the deck door, his slender frame hunched under the heavy bag.

Lugging the black bag down the deck steps, catching every other loose nail in the wooden planks along the way, Miles noticed red and blue flashing lights on the next street over. He dropped the bag next to the overflowing tin trash can and looked at the lights once more to see if he could pinpoint exactly where they were coming from. Suddenly, a gunshot rang out.

Jumping in shock, Miles stumbled over his own feet,

crashing onto the pile of trash. The plastic forks and folded plates poked and pried at his skin through the bag. He stood and dashed to the door, his hands fumbling to open it.

Once inside, Miles quickly locked it. Turning to tell his parents what he had heard, he found them frozen like statues, eyes glued to the television.

"What's going on?" he asked.

Elaine quickly shushed him.

Miles locked his eyes on the screen to see what had transfixed his parents.

It can't be.

"Riots in the streets downtown," he heard the anchor say, and the rest was a jumble until he got to the words, "Stay inside."

"Not another riot." Miles sighed, plopping down on the couch next to his father. Then to his mother, he added: "Was it another Black man who got shot?"

He wondered whether the gunshot he heard outside would soon be discussed live.

Elaine's fingernails were soon to be nubs the way she bit them. "This police brutality needs to stop. It's like they think every Black person is a born criminal. I wish racism would end already."

"Shush!" Rodger said, using the remote to increase the volume on the television. "I don't think anyone was shot this time. I think it's something different."

While Elaine, Miles, and Rodger listened in, the station network went live to a reporter stationed downtown.

The reporter, standing outside in the cold in front of

UW Medical Center, Northwest, discussed what appeared to be a new virus: "There have been thirty confirmed cases within the last two days, all patients showing similar symptoms." He put his finger up to his ear as he listened to what the network was telling him. "Reports say the root cause of the outbreak appears to be tainted crops and livestock originating from multiple farms in the area."

The reporter checked his surroundings and described what he saw: "Many people are rioting, blaming the government due to the regulations on farming with pesticides, which in turn resulted in many falling ill to what *seems* like the flu." The camera panned over hundreds of bystanders, some holding signs, marching in the middle of the street. Miles spotted a couple of people on camera spraying graffiti, and it appeared that small groups blocked the entrances to some storefronts and businesses.

The reporter approached an outraged civilian and asked him if there were any concerns he'd like to address. The elderly Asian man, speaking in a heavy accent and broken English, didn't hesitate to say what was on his mind. He leaned in closer to the microphone in the reporter's hand as the cameraman inched closer. "Two days ago I got fresh veggies for my dog. But he didn't want. He sniffed and sniffed, then turned away. Why? I ask myself. For a long time, he eat fresh veggies, now he won't go near them. Now I ask myself—"

Their conversation got cut short. Lights flashed across the television screen as Miles and his parents watched. The reporter quickly signaled the old man to *hold that thought* as he rushed over to the side of the hospital to catch the arriving patient.

Could it be another possible case of the flu? The ambulance came to a screeching halt as two nursing staff members rushed out the sliding glass doors of the emergency room entrance, a gurney, and other life-saving equipment rolling by their side. The cameraman managed to get a shot through the back window of the ambulance, giving viewers a glimpse of an EMT performing CPR on the patient until a nurse insisted he step away from the vehicle.

He stepped back, but just then, the ambulance doors burst open, providing another clear view inside the truck. This time, the camera caught the audio of hospital personnel discussing a possible connection between the man's symptoms and the food he had eaten. The camera focused in on the patient just as he flatlined. Viewers watched as the EMTs placed an oxygen mask on the man, injected some sort of medicine intravenously, then grabbed the defibrillator and sent a shock through his body. His pulse didn't resume.

They tried to resuscitate the man for a second time, but still, there was no pulse. Miles watched as the EMT and nurse called the time of death, live on television. The cameraman turned toward the reporter, who simply looked at his viewers in stunned silence for a moment before the network cut back to the studio.

The Winstead family was at a loss for words as the news anchor tried his best to reassure the network's viewers. "The excruciating footage we've just witnessed confirms how serious this flu-like sickness is. Please look over your perishables, report to the nearest urgent care if you show any signs of sickness, and please... stay safe."

"Well, at least it wasn't another Black man who got shot," Elaine said.

"But this does seem serious," Rodger added.

Miles's heart rate began to increase, his fears of the unknown taking over. "I think I need another pill." He shot up from the couch and headed for the kitchen.

"Now, Miles," Elaine said, crossing her arms and shifting her weight to one hip, "your prescription's already stretched thin. We don't want you running out again."

Rodger peered over the backrest of the loveseat. "Yeah, last time was hell."

Miles remembered the last time he ran out of pills. *I can't do that again. Three weeks was unbearable.*

Three weeks it took for his parents to afford a refill on his prescription. In the meantime, he struggled to function properly, unable to communicate even with his parents. He didn't sleep, barely ate, and eventually didn't even leave the house. He had a hell of a lot of schoolwork to make up afterward. His parents were right. Best to go easy on the Xanax.

"Well, I guess it's goodnight then." Kissing his mother on the cheek and exchanging hugs with his father, he headed to the bathroom to take a quick shower, then hopped into bed.

As Miles lay in his room, staring up at the ever-growing crack in his ceiling, he thought about the gunshot he had heard earlier. *Could it have been a perp on the run? A car's exhaust backfiring? No, that doesn't explain the lights. A rabid animal? Maybe it was a werewolf. If the gun had silver bullets, it could have been a werewolf. Or maybe it was a zombie. Do bullets kill zombies? Come on, Miles, don't be stupid. Well, whatever it is, I hope it's nothing serious.*

This hadn't been Miles's first time hearing a gunshot. He loved movies, especially ones that involved gun violence. He'd even tried shooting one—*tried* being the operative word. His father had brought him into the woods to teach him the art of trapping and hunting not long before he met Alice. Sadly, anxiety had prevented Miles from excelling in that field, but at least he'd white-knuckled through enough instruction to be able to say he was familiar with the trade.

———

FIFTEEN MINUTES after the live news broadcast from the hospital had ended, the cameraman and reporter packed up the last of their equipment and loaded it into the van.

"Hurry up, Ralph, let's get outta here," Eric, the reporter said.

A woman's scream pealed out from the direction of the ambulance. They both turned to look, but it was Eric who first spotted something unusual—something he had seen only in a movie. He immediately signaled Ralph to set the camera back up to catch what could possibly make the morning news.

"Hurry! I don't want to miss it!"

Sweat beaded up on Ralph's forehead as he frantically

pulled a handheld out of its case. "I'm coming, I'm coming! I'm moving as fast I can." He turned on the camera, hit the record button, and swung the lens toward the back of the ambulance. His eyes grew wide. "What the hell is that?"

Eric shuddered at the unsightly scene. The patient that had died in the back of the ambulance now sat up on the gurney, his torso and head stirring subtly.

"Get closer," Eric urged Ralph.

"Na-uh," Ralph said. "You wanna get in there, be my guest. I'll zoom right in from here."

"Hell no! Fine, just zoom in to see if you can catch his face."

Had they resuscitated the man on the gurney? Eric, a science nerd, had read a few studies claiming that the human brain can survive for a fair amount of time without oxygen. Had this man been successfully brought back to life?

Eric glanced at the woman who had screamed upon finding the man still alive. "You okay miss?" The woman in the attendant uniform didn't say a word. Didn't look at him, either. She didn't even quake in her clogs. She couldn't have been more frozen if she'd just laid eyes on Medusa.

A security guard arrived seconds later to make sure everything was okay. Ralph kept recording, not wanting to miss a thing, catching everyone's expressions on camera. "We're both getting raises after this," he whispered. Then he turned his focus back toward the ambulance.

There the man sat, his pale skin dull in the shadows of the truck, the whites of his eyes dark with some unfathomable emotion, his voice mute. He had begun to emit a horrid stench as if he had evacuated his bowels.

Eric held his breath as both the attendant and security guard inched toward the animated body. The putrid smell intensified, and they struggled not to gag. The woman touched the gurney first, sending a pulse of energy through the metal and up to the straps that held the man's legs in place.

That slight vibration was all it took to rouse the patient from his stupor. In a single, sudden movement, he lunged toward the woman, grabbed her hand, pulled her toward him, and sunk his teeth deep into her forearm. She screamed and tried to pull away, but the man didn't release his deathly grip on her. He simply continued with his work of tearing the flesh from her arm, dragging some tendons along with it.

Eric gasped as he watched the security guard struggle to separate the woman from the beast. Finally, he was able to put words to his racing thoughts. "Ohh shit, it's a fucking zombie!"

Ralph almost dropped the camera. "We gotta go."

"The hell we do!" Eric shot back. "We're getting all of this!" He could already see his Pulitzer sitting on his desk. On his much bigger desk in his much, much hotter market.

"You do you." Ralph tossed Eric the camera. "I'm out." He huffed and puffed back to the truck, got in, and drove off, leaving Eric alone to capture the last days of humanity... or to die trying.

4

"Good morning," Rodger said, his face buried in the Sunday comics. He sat at the kitchen dinette.

"Morning," Miles said, sleepily scratching at the back of his head. "You find any job listings? Figured I'd get looking." He opened the food pantry and picked out a box of cereal.

"A few things, but nothing you'd want to do."

Grabbing a bowl and some milk, Miles noticed his mother's absence. Despite his hunger, he put his breakfast supplies down on the table and took a minute to look for her. He stepped into the living area and found her anxiously staring out the window near the front door, a cup of coffee pressed against her lips.

"When's the last time you checked on her?" Miles asked his father, leaning against the doorjamb dividing the living area and kitchen.

The paper in Rodger's hands didn't budge an inch. "Thirty minutes ago. She's fine."

Shrugging off his father's reply, Miles approached her. "I guess I'm not the only one who's anxious," he said, coming up behind her.

Elaine sighed, not breaking focus on the neighbor across the street. Miles joined her in watching the middle-aged man unload case after case of bottled water and canned goods from his SUV's trunk. "All those years of counseling and I still feel like I have no control," she said.

Miles rubbed her shoulder. "Mom, you've done better than me."

"But it still lingers, Miles."

He scoffed. "At least you don't have to take meds anymore. You've worked really hard, and it's paid off. Your anxiety only flares up in times of crisis these days. Mine still flares up over split milk." This elicited the smile Miles was hoping for. "C'mon, how about you join us at the table?" Elaine followed Miles back into the kitchen.

As Miles poured himself a bowl of cereal, Elaine placed her empty mug in the sink. But instead of taking a seat at the dinette, as Miles had suggested, she approached her husband, leaned down close to his ear, and whispered something softly enough that Miles couldn't hear.

Miles may not have heard what his mother said, but he could tell in an instant that whatever it was, his father didn't like it. Rodger closed the paper abruptly and folded it in half with a scowl.

"Honey, we can't afford to—"

"I don't care," Elaine interrupted. "We have to make

sure there's plenty of food just in case things get hectic. It's called thinking ahead!"

"You heard the news broadcaster. He said stay inside. I'm sticking to that. We don't need to visit the grocery store."

Miles knew his mother wouldn't take no for an answer. But he also knew his father wouldn't want to spend the extra cash on stockpiling groceries just for them to sit on the shelf for weeks.

"If you don't go, then Miles and I will go," Elaine said.

"Oh yeah? I don't see that happening." Skepticism weighed heavy in Rodger's tone.

"C'mon, Miles, let's go." Elaine reached for his hand.

Miles jerked away before she could grab hold. "Right now? No way. I just started eating." Miles held up a spoonful of cereal to make his point.

She glanced at the digital clock on the stove. It read a quarter after nine. "Fine. Eat. But if we don't get a move on soon, the stores will get crowded."

"That's if they're not *already* crowded," Rodger added.

"Even when I'm done, I'm not going," Miles said.

Rodger looked at Miles, then back at Elaine. "I guess you're going by yourself, then."

"C'mon, Mom, don't go. It'll be safer if you stay here. There's no telling what craziness is going on downtown."

"Well, if you two want to starve, then be my guest, but I don't want to be the neighbor that begs for food when the stores run out."

"That's *if* they run out, Elaine," Rodger added.

Looking at how his mother fiercely gripped herself,

Miles could tell she was seriously concerned for the future. And in this case, he couldn't help but feel that the source of her agitation—last night's report about the deadly virus—was justified. But did his father see it that way? Miles didn't want his family to suffer if people were to start dropping like flies around them. Maybe his mother had a point.

"Still want to hit the store, Mom?" Miles asked after he'd finished his bowl of cereal.

"You'll come?" Elaine replied, her face lighting up with a smile.

"Even though I don't want to, I will."

"Fine," Rodger threw his palms up in surrender. "How about we all just go and get it over with? I don't think we should, but since when does it matter what I think?" He stood from the table. "I'll get the keys."

As Rodger disappeared, Miles sprinted upstairs to brush his teeth, then returned to the downstairs closet to retrieve his sneakers. Elaine was the first out the front door, followed by Miles. They were still standing by the Ford Ranger, waiting for Rodger to arrive with the keys to unlock it, when Miles remembered he'd forgotten something important.

"I'll be right back," Miles said, heading back toward the house.

"Forget your meds again?" she asked.

"Yep!"

Miles hurried up the stone walkway onto the creaky wooden porch. Just as he reached for the handle on the front door, Rodger opened it, and Miles's heart skipped a beat—

not just from the surprise but also from the vision before him: his father, carrying a .357 Magnum.

"You worried something might happen?" Miles asked, barely able to get the words out.

"You can never be too prepared," Rodger said. As his father brushed past him, Miles could hear a few extra rounds jiggling in his jeans pocket.

Miles tried to block what he had seen from his thoughts as his breathing thickened. He rushed to the medicine cabinet in the kitchen to grab his bottle of pills, then reached with a shaking hand for a glass from another cabinet. Filling the glass with water from the tap, he tossed the Xanax in his mouth and gave it a chase, instantly feeling a sense of relief.

Miles knew it took more than just a few seconds for Xanax to actually kick in. But at this point, he found solace in the act of taking the pill, not in the effects of the medication itself. If his parents were to swap his medication for placebos to save money, he wondered if he'd even notice. He placed the glass in the sink and returned to the truck.

———

THEY DROVE past neighborhood after neighborhood, making their way into the city, each mile they went becoming more and more congested with traffic and pedestrians. The myriad of protesters that had amassed from all over sent frightening chills down Miles's spine. Many held signs that read STOP LYING TO US and HOW MANY MORE

HAVE TO DIE? Others displayed unpleasant derogatory slurs directed toward the government and its cohorts.

"Oh my," Elaine said, eyes darting left and right at all the people standing on the sidewalks and gathering on corners.

"Told you," Rodger said. "We should've stayed inside."

Traffic lights and intersections clogged with demonstrators kept the Winstead family moving at a snail's pace. Roars from the people echoed in the streets, sending an earthquake-like vibration through the ground; a constant pulse for every step a rioter took.

"This doesn't look anything like the last riot," Miles said warily.

"Sure doesn't." Rodger couldn't agree more.

Miles continued looking out the window, focusing on controlling his heart rate the best he could as large numbers of people yelled words he couldn't quite decipher over muffling megaphones. They threw rotten food at police officers. Storefronts were covered in the tainted goods, drawing flies and maggots to swarm the entrances. God, was it a shit show. No amount of recalls could have prevented this.

Suddenly, the car stopped, sending Miles's forehead smashing into the back of the passenger seat's headrest.

"C'mon, Dad!" He rubbed his forehead.

"Sorry," Rodger said, peering back at Miles through the rearview mirror. "But I'll be damned if we fall victim to a life-savings-draining lawsuit because some ignorant rioter decided to jump out in front of us."

Miles hadn't wanted to leave the house. Hadn't wanted

his parents to, either. He'd agreed with his father when it came to going out: it was a bad idea. But he'd been afraid to let his mother go alone, afraid she could get hurt with no one there to help.

Now, Miles was seeing firsthand just how bad this idea was. He saw it in the look on his father's face as he glanced over at his wife in the passenger seat, witnessing her uneasiness. He saw it in his mother's sweat-drenched forehead, her eyes darting left and right out of each window at the roaring crowd. He saw it on the faces of those in the angry mob, some rocking nearby cars, others sporting weapons ranging from guns and knives to bats and masonry bricks. Anything they could get their hands on.

The steady tapping of Elaine's leg on the thick rubber floor mat and the sound of her nails scraping at the denim on her jeans confirmed what Miles suspected: his mother was lost in panic. He wondered whether she had the presence of mind to think about what a nightmare it would have been for her to try to make it through this alone. Regardless, the family was together, and there was no turning back now. They were out, vulnerable, miles away from home.

A traffic light turned red, and the Ford Ranger eased to a stop about a block from the courthouse. Ullman's grocer was finally in sight from where they sat. They just had to wait for the signal to turn green.

A BLOCK from where the Winstead family sat waiting for the light to change, a rioter in the crowd sweated profusely. He marched to the same tune as everyone else, yelling and tossing expired vegetables at officers who posed as crowd control.

"You don't look so good, man," a fellow protester said, noticing the man's pale skin and weak stance.

He wiped the sweat from his brow. "I'm okay. Just a little hot, that's all." He stepped closer, sifting through the crowd until he reached the front, coming face-to-face with the line of officers wielding riot shields.

"Get back!" one officer shouted. "Get back!"

The man didn't listen. He tossed a few rotten tomatoes over the shields, and all three landed on the courthouse steps. The officer attempted to shove the man backward, away from the front of the crowd, by pushing him with his shield. Instead, he smacked the man in the head, and his unconscious body fell to the ground in front of the crowd.

"What the hell, man?!" a male protester yelled. "You can't do that to us!"

"Get back!" the officer shouted once more.

"Fuck you!" another protester answered.

"Yeah, fuck you, pig!" a woman's voice called out.

Many more voices began shouting as a young woman went to help the unconscious man. She attempted to wake him, but the man didn't come to. She checked his pulse, but when she felt nothing, she gasped, almost falling back on her ass. She jumped up and approached the officer, getting as close as she could without getting hit herself.

"This man needs immediate medical assistance. Call an ambulance!" she yelled.

The officer repeated himself, his voice muffled by his face mask and shield.

"The man is dead!" She pointed to the man on the ground behind her.

"Get back!" the officer repeated once more. "If he's dead, he's in no need of assistance."

"What are you talking about? He still needs—" The girl turned to find the man she had checked on slowly getting up. She hurried back to help him stand, but as soon as she was within arms length, the man reached up, latched onto her wrist, and took a bite out of her ankle. The surrounding crowd watched the horrifying scene unfold as the young woman screamed out a mixture of pain, shock, and fear.

"What the fuck?!" someone shouted.

The people in front started sprinting toward the back of the crowd, trying to escape the devilish ghoul. Others rushed the officers, hoping to take advantage of the chaos to gain some ground against law enforcement.

The girl's skin tore from her shin as the man rose to his feet. Then, still chewing the mouthful of flesh, he set his sights on the officer who had caused his fatal injury.

"Get back! I repeat, get back! I won't say it again." The officer readjusted himself behind his shield, preparing to shove the man once more.

Though the man had made it to his feet, he stood slightly crooked, his body leaning on one hip more than the other. His eyes had taken on a dull, grey hue, and his jaw slacked open, allowing a steady stream of drool to escape. The drool was red with blood, remnants of the girl's flesh still lodged in his teeth.

Suddenly, the man lunged at the officer, gluing himself onto the shield.

The officer studied the man's eyes before shoving him to the ground again. "That's it." He pulled out his service pistol and aimed it at the man. "I will use this if you don't stay back!"

The man stood and lunged at the officer once more.

———

THE SOUND of a gunshot sent Miles's cortisol levels through the roof. His eyes exploded in fear as many protesters began screaming in terror—others in anger. Many people ran, tripping and stumbling over one another as they scattered like a pack of gazelles when they spot a lion. Miles, now crouched down low in the backseat, carefully peeked out every window until he could figure out what had happened. He found his answer dead ahead: an officer had shot a violent protester.

As some fled the scene, others took to the police, pouncing on them like a cat on a mouse. The block had turned into a war zone. Bodies were being tackled left and right as a dead body lay flat on the ground in the middle of the street. No amount of medicine could have prepared Miles for what he had seen. Police readied their pistols and tasers as they tried their best to defend themselves against the rushing mob of pedestrians.

The light turned green, but Rodger's foot didn't budge. The car behind them honked its horn, but still, he didn't move.

"Go, Dad!" Miles shouted, realizing the light had changed.

But they didn't go anywhere. At the sound of gunfire, all hell had broken loose. To move a vehicle an inch among the crowd would only stir them up more and increase the chance of an incident breaking out between them and the protesters. The kind of incident that could only be defused by Rodger's Magnum.

In other words, they were stuck.

The officer that shot the man had hit him directly in the chest, sending a bullet right through his heart and inciting a war. The sick man didn't stand a chance. Though only minutes had passed, it seemed clear the crowd would soon give itself over fully to bloodshed.

"Honey, we need to leave," Elaine said, placing her hand on Rodger's thigh.

"I had a feeling this would happen." Rodger pulled the .357 from his pocket and placed his foot gently on the accelerator pedal, inching the pickup forward.

By this time, Miles's chest was so tight he couldn't breathe. Every ounce of adrenaline in his body coursed through his veins now. Despite the Xanax in his system, he was in a full-blown state of panic, leaving him squeezing at the edges of his seat with a vise-like grip as he watched in terror.

As Miles watched the rioters protect themselves against the police using their signs, bits of masonry bricks, and guns, he noticed something in the distance. Through the chaos of the crowd, he caught a glimpse of the man who had been shot by the officer. The man whose death had started the chaos around him. Only instead of lying on the ground, he was sitting bolt upright, staring directly back at Miles.

Had the man worn a vest? Had the bullet somehow missed his heart? Even if it did, it surely would have punctured a lung.

Am I dreaming? Miles rubbed his eyes to check. He wasn't. He looked again, then shuddered. His heart stopped. Pulling at his shirt collar—trying so desperately to breathe— his lungs shrank to a fourth of their usual size. He choked.

"We need to go, now!" he managed to get out.

The man who had been miraculously brought back to life struggled to stand and ultimately succeeded by latching his lifeless arms onto another protester.

"Jesus," Rodger said, amazed at the chaos around him. "This is what happens when they poison our food." He shook his head. "Who would've thought?"

Rather than answer his father's rhetorical question, Miles managed to spit out the words necessary to point out the man that had been shot to his parents. Both gasped as they took in the ghastly sight. Even from a distance, they could see he wasn't right: his body was partially hunched, and his movements were slow and wobbly like a drunk.

Miles thought his mannerisms looked almost animalistic like he was a hunter searching for prey in the wild.

For once, both Rodger and Elaine agreed with Miles that this was a good time to panic. Rodger lay his hand heavy on the horn, deafening people inches from his pickup. As the truck crept forward and to the left, Miles rocked back and forth in his seat, trying his best to remain calm. The Ford took blow after blow as cops slammed rioters against the truck's body to overpower them. One even landed in the truck bed, then jumped out.

A second later, someone opened Elaine's door but quickly lost grip of the handle, allowing her to slam it closed and lock it. Rodger tried to do the same, but it was too late. Someone had opened his door before he had the chance to push the lock pin. They yanked him out of the cabin and slammed him against the side of his truck, his safety belt keeping him wedged between the door and jamb. His revolver had fallen out of his lap during the brawl, landing in the driver's seat.

As the truck continued creeping forward, Elaine reached for the gun, aimed, and pulled the trigger. Miles's ears popped like a cork from the shot in such a confined space. Blood splattered back on Rodger's navy shirt. The man that had pulled him from the truck had taken a bullet to the shoulder. He fell back, loosening his grip on Rodger. Elaine dropped the Smith & Wesson back into the center console.

Rodger turned and punched the guy who had grabbed him, landing a vicious blow to his jaw. Then he unbuckled his seatbelt and reached for his gun. Before he could spin around to defend himself, however, an officer mistook him for a rioter, catching Rodger in a chokehold with his nightstick.

Rodger elbowed the cop in the chest, cracking his funny bone against a bullet-proof vest. "Shit!"

Elaine tried to grab the gun again but was thrown off guard when a brick flew in through the passenger window, shattering it and sending glass shards cascading over her body. "No! Stop it!" She struggled to defend herself against another rioter making his way in. It wasn't long, however, before Elaine got pulled out the missing window and thrown to the ground by an aggravated rioter. She struggled to break free from the man's grasp.

Miles's hands trembled in fear, and his vision blurred from the sweat pouring down his forehead. Desperate to help his parents, he reached for the revolver in the center console, aimed it, and fired.

5

Rodger had been shot. A .357 mag bullet had entered his face through his jaw and exited out the base of his skull. Blood splatter covered the face of the officer who had been choking him with his nightstick a split second before.

Miles almost fainted at the sight of his father's body collapsing to the ground. It was an image he knew he would never be able to forget—a nightmare that would forever haunt him.

He dropped the gun in shock. Miles froze, panicked and afraid, his mind jumbled with failed attempts to organize and interpret the events of the last hour. He receded into the fetal position in the back seat, unable to acknowledge anything but his own feelings of guilt and shame. *What've I done? What've I done? What've I done?*

Miles's inner chant was interrupted by the voice of the

blood-covered officer, who had climbed into the now-empty driver's seat of the pickup.

"Get out!" he demanded, loudly and harshly, as though Miles were the one intruding upon a space that did not belong to him.

Miles opened his eyes just as the officer grabbed the revolver that Miles himself had let fall between the two front seats. He pointed it toward the backseat and repeated his demand, even louder this time, but Miles didn't budge. Miles's lack of response did not come from any conscious intention to stand his ground, but rather from being in a state of shock. He had retreated deep into his subconscious mind. Time was still, frozen, as he pondered the irony of the fact that he was now at the end of the barrel of the very same gun with which he had just killed his father. It was perfect, in a way, the symmetry of it...

Miles expected to hear a gunshot ring out then, but instead, he heard the officer cry out in pain. The unexpected sound snapped Miles back into what appeared to be reality, only it didn't resemble any reality Miles had encountered before. He immediately identified the source of the officer's pain. The man's neck was torn to shreds, and blood spurted out of his throat like water from an open fire hydrant. A creature had bitten him in the jugular, and whatever it was, it was pulling him out of the car and down to the ground, drenching the inside of the car door with blood as he went.

This isn't real. It's just a nightmare.

Miles closed his eyes, covered his ears, and pulled his knees even closer toward his chest, trying to escape the screams roaring outside. *This isn't real. It's just a nightmare.* Something crashed against the truck, nearly knocking him off the backseat and interrupting his mantra.

"Miles! Grab my hand," Elaine shouted. She'd finally freed herself of the angry protesters determined to teach her family a lesson for driving through their demonstration, and she leaned across the passenger seat to extend her hand to Miles over the center console.

Miles didn't move.

"Hurry, Miles!"

The sound of fear in his mother's voice roused Miles from his stupor; he quickly stumbled over the console, climbed over the passenger seat, and fell into his mother's arms.

"Where's your father?" she asked, her voice sounding frantic.

Miles couldn't answer.

"Where's your father?" Elaine asked again, this time holding onto Miles's shoulders and looking him straight in the eyes.

Tears rolled down Miles's cheeks, but he remained silent. Shock once again began to take over. Grabbing his hand, Elaine leaned back into the vehicle to search for the .357 Magnum. Miles knew she wouldn't find the gun; it had fallen out of the truck along with the bloody officer. What she would find, however, was his father's body, lying dead on the ground below the driver-side door.

"Oh no," she said. Miles watched her body stiffen across the truck's front seats.

She slowly backed herself out of the cabin and turned back to Miles. "What happened?"

Miles had to confess his mistake. It was his fault his father had died. It was his own inability to stay calm that had killed him. But even before the words came out, he couldn't bear the shock on his mother's face. The way she fell back and dropped to her knees. Remorse filled his veins as he watched his mother mourn the loss of her husband. She let out deep sobs of pain.

As Miles stood mute and defenseless against his thoughts, someone bumped him, knocking him to the ground. With Elaine's attention, too, focused elsewhere, that person was easily able to hop into the truck, put it in reverse, and drive off, leaving both of them stranded.

It suddenly struck Miles with devastating clarity that he and his mother were still in grave danger. "Mom!" He tugged at her arms, trying to pull her up from her knees. "Mom! We gotta go. We're not safe!"

———

IT ONLY TOOK a few hours for the city to break down into anarchy. The once quiet, lush streets of Seattle turned into a hectic battlefield ruled by the doctrine of "every person for themselves." Many sat out on their front porches ready to protect what was rightfully theirs; others took to the streets, looting and robbing as they went. Fires burned everywhere, sending clouds of smoke across the cityscape.

Meanwhile, the number of undead continued to climb in the misty shadows of the city.

Miles and Elaine kept their arms linked together and their heads down as they began their long journey home, hoping to avoid drawing any more unnecessary attention to themselves. Still, Miles could not stop repeating his mantra under his breath.

"This isn't happening. This isn't real. This isn't happening. This isn't real."

Elaine shushed him.

"Maybe it is real. Maybe it's all my fault."

"God dammit, Miles! Do you ever shut up?" Elaine grabbed at her head with her free hand, agitation weighing heavy on her mind. Miles fell silent and hung his head down even further, and the gesture tugged at Elaine's already broken heart. "I just need to think," she said gently, stopping to take note of what street they were on.

An explosion erupted nearby, strong enough to shake the ground beneath them.

"Shit!" Miles muttered, but whatever came out of his mouth after that was drowned out by the sound of screeching tires.

Elaine pulled Miles by the arm until they were both positioned behind a nearby car, hidden from view of whoever may be approaching in a speeding vehicle. Within seconds a convertible Jeep with its top down whizzed past them and came to a halt near an ATM at the end of the block. Three men, all armed with assault rifles, jumped out, and a fourth remained behind the wheel.

"What the hell?" Miles whispered.

Elaine shushed him again.

He could feel his mother's heartbeat and sense her fear from the way her body quivered against his. He watched as the men attached a chain to the ATM, then to the rear of the Jeep.

"No, what are you doing?" Elaine muttered under her breath.

An elderly gentleman from inside the bank stepped out and approached the three men. Miles couldn't make out what they were saying. But whatever it was, it didn't last long. One man readied his rifle and sent ten rounds into the bank employee, leaving his body to collapse under itself. Then all three men jumped back in the Jeep and sped off, yanking the ATM from the wall as they went. The screeching sounds of tearing metal followed as they dragged the machine down the street and out of sight.

Elaine gasped. "Oh my God."

She covered her mouth, pressing her back against the cold metal car they hid behind. She held Miles tight as he covered his ringing ears.

Suddenly, as if she'd just remembered something important, Elaine grabbed Miles's hand and continued onward, rushing right past the lifeless body of the old man that had been shot. There was nothing they could do for him, and if they kept moving, they had a chance of making it home before nightfall.

<hr>

AN HOUR LATER, Miles and Elaine finally made it back home from their morning supply run with no supplies, no pickup truck, and no Rodger. The old wooden planks creaked under their feet as they climbed the front porch. Miles watched his mother struggle to insert the key into the door's lock.

"You okay, Mom?" he asked.

Elaine started tearing up again. "I'm fine."

She continued struggling until Miles grabbed her bloody hand and held it steady enough to slide the key into the keyhole. When the door finally opened, the two rushed inside and quickly locked the door behind them, attaching the bolt lock above the handle and sliding the loveseat over from the living area to use as reinforcement.

Miles wandered back into the living area and turned on the television. He watched the local news channel ring its emergency broadcast, airing health and safety protocols as his mother ventured into the kitchen.

Alice!

Miles fished his cell phone out of his pocket and frantically dialed his girlfriend's number, but the line just rang and rang. No answer, not even voicemail. He hit redial and still got nothing.

Dammit!

The sound of sobbing drew Miles toward the kitchen to check on his mother. When he peeked his head around the corner, he saw her taking deep breaths, probably to calm her sporadic heart rate. She peered out the window over the kitchen sink and exhaled, resting her hands on the edge of the counter.

"If I hadn't tried to think ahead, maybe you'd still be here," she muttered under her breath. She clenched her fists and stared at her faint reflection in the windowpane.

"It's not your fault, Mom," Miles said. He walked across the kitchen and stood next to her at the counter. "It's all my fault. It's my fault, Mom. And I'm sorry."

Just then, a fiery shock shot down Elaine's leg, causing her to wince in pain so violently her entire body jolted upright. When she reached down to squeeze at her Achille's, her hand brushed against a gooey substance on her jeans. When she brought her fingers up to examine them, she found them coated in pasty, half-dried blood.

"You're bleeding?" Miles asked. "When'd you get hurt?"

She looked at Miles with a confused expression. "I don't know." She quickly limped to the hall bathroom and sat on the commode, with Miles following closely behind. Unlacing her left shoe, Elaine rolled up her pants leg and slid off her bloody tube sock to find a few teeth marks above her ankle.

Miles gasped. *Where could they have come from? God, I hope she didn't get bit by that thing that got the officer!*

"That looks like a bite mark."

Elaine tried to recount all the steps she had taken so far, mumbling nonsense as she did so. "It can't be. I didn't get bit. A person would remember getting bit. Wouldn't you think, Miles?"

They'd gone through a lot that day, though, and things

happened so fast out there—too quickly for her or Miles to recollect everything. Miles knew there were gaps in his timeline that would probably never be filled. But to forget something like that? Surely she couldn't have. Or did she?

At that moment, thoughts of the sickness flooded Miles's mind: fever, chills, diarrhea, vomit, fatigue. What else had he learned from the network's broadcast?

"Do you feel any different?" Miles asked.

Elaine glanced up at him. "Do I *feel* any different?" she repeated thoughtfully, as though she'd never heard those five words used together before. "Miles, I can't feel a thing right now."

Her loss of feeling was to be expected. After the trauma of the day's events, her body, like Miles's own, had to have undergone a depletion of adrenaline.

He didn't know for sure exactly whether his mother had contracted the sickness, but what he did know was that she could only protect him for so long before he'd eventually be all alone—left to fend for himself in a world full of inconceivable danger.

2

LOST
&
FOUND

Six Months Later

JOURNAL ENTRY #43:
FRIDAY, DECEMBER 8TH, 2023

I never would've thought the summer after graduation would last forever. It's been six months since it happened. The *Great Reset* I call it. I never would've thought that that'd be the last time I'd see them, let alone lead a normal life. Honestly, I'm surprised I've managed to survive this long. Every day I wake up, wondering if it'll be my last.

It only took a week for my mother to die. Seven days exactly. When she started to show signs, it was too late. That night after the riot—as a precaution—it was agreed that she'd remain locked in her bedroom for my safety. Maybe she thought I couldn't handle killing her if she tried biting me. But what could I do? Even though I didn't want her locked up, she still remained in her room. It was her choice. And as days went on, the virus spread through her body like wildfire.

To be honest, I don't even think they're in a better place now. And it's all my fault. It only took three weeks for the world to burn. Luxuries like toilet paper and food were the first to go, then commodities like gasoline went next. People ran the pumps dry just to have fuel for vehicles. But nobody could go anywhere. Highways were barricaded and sanctioned by the military, preventing many from leveling the city, as if to quarantine us.

Communications were the next to go. The government cut all communication networks on the third day; no internet, no cell phones, and no television. Couldn't even receive radio broadcasts. Yeah, there were a few channels on AM that some conspirators would broadcast from every now and then, but after a few weeks of listening to them, I realized they had no interest in banding together other survivors. So I stopped listening. No reason to give myself false hope.

So now I'm back to being alone. God, do I hate being alone. Not much time to worry about that now though. These days, survival's all that matters. That was the only thing that ever did I guess. The virus created thousands of monsters, and now they're running rampant in the streets. Or at least they were. I haven't seen many of them lately. The Silent Ones, I call them. Maybe they're dying off. I don't really know, exactly. All I know is that times are different, and things are scarce. I just hope the way things are now won't last forever. And if they do, then God help us all.

I started this journal to leave something behind for whoever finds it in case I die 'cause I really don't know how much more I can take. I've lost everything at this point: my family, the love of my life, myself. But if these are the last days of civilization, then maybe no one will ever get to read this. Maybe writing this whole thing is pointless. Maybe I should just kill myself.

Sincerely, M.W.

P.S. Alice if you're somewhere out there and ever find this, just know that I loved you so much. xoxo

6

Miles's heart skipped a beat as a black bear stood on its hind legs and let out a huge, angry roar. He had trekked too close to the den where the mother's newborn cubs lay. Miles knew better than to hike up the mountain through the woods instead of walking along the highway, but how else would he reach the cabin in time for nightfall? The temperature had already dropped ten degrees within the last hour. It would only get colder as the sun continued to set.

Miles's heart dropped to the pit of his stomach as he stared dead at the beast. *Stay calm, you've got this. No sudden moves.*

As the bear fell back on all fours and tucked her head, he knew exactly what was coming next. He had seen enough of *National Geographic* to know when to cut his losses. Taking a deep breath, Miles turned and ran, taking long strides with his long legs. The bear planted her front feet into the leafy mud and charged. Miles had already managed a twelve-foot lead by the time she had moved, but that would quickly diminish and be recouped by her rapid speed—thirty-five miles per hour compared to his feeble ten. But what he lacked in physical agility he sure made up for in brains.

Miles jumped over a water puddle as the bear blazed right through it. He dashed past one tree, another, then took a sudden right turn, hoping she wouldn't catch on.

Gotta keep moving! Gotta keep moving!

He spotted the large stream he had crossed on his way up the mountain. If he could make it across, maybe—just maybe—she'd give up on chasing him. Miles leaped over a huge tree that had recently fallen, slapping the tip of his boot against the trunk. He crashed to the ground, almost breaking his wrist upon impact as he tried to brace himself.

Shit!

Rolling over, he laid flat, wedging himself deep into the mud as far under the tree as he could, hoping the bear didn't see where he had landed.

One, two, three, breathe. One, two, three, breathe. One, two three... His rampant heart rate slowed as he felt the deep thud of the creature's presence. Sensing her heavy feet and breathing with every trudge she took, Miles didn't budge an inch. She cleared her nose and snarled.

Please just leave. Please just leave. Please just leave.

Miles closed his eyes and stayed as still as he possibly could, aware that if he had made even the slightest noise, not even the nine-hundred-pound log standing between him and this giant force of nature could protect him from utter death.

All he could hear in the silence of the forest were the calming sounds of mother nature: chirping crickets in the distance, the current of the nearby stream, rustling leaves against the evening breeze.

Miles felt the bear could sense his fear, his frantic pulse beating through the ground. Could probably smell his stench, too, since he was in desperate need of a shower. She began to paw at the log he was seeking shelter behind, bringing it to rock back and forth. A few drops of rain pelted his glasses, then his forehead, and before he knew it, the rain had turned into a torrential downpour, leaving him drenched. The bear nudged the log once more, let out a retreating roar, then turned and trudged off back to her dwelling to care for her newborn cubs, leaving Miles to soak in a puddle of sweat, fear, and rainwater.

For Miles, there was no better feeling. He had survived his first ever bear attack, and he had done so without falling victim to his handicap. It was surely another step in conquering his anxiety—to become strong and fearless. Still, he was far from not ever needing to take a pill again. Standing, trying his best not to stumble over and fall back into the mud, Miles realized that his bear encounter had cost him more daylight than he'd had to spare. The sun had come and gone. His eyes struggled to adjust to the darkness. He may have conquered Mama Bear, but now he faced a new danger: finding a place to sleep for the night.

Why did you have to pick a place in the middle of

nowhere, Miles? Oh yeah, that's right, so no one will find you. He kicked at the mud beneath his feet.

Throughout the first few weeks of the outbreak, the military did regular perimeter checks, rounding up survivors to put in camps. At first, the idea of being taken in by the government, with the free food and medical supplies that implied, was somewhat appealing to Miles. But soon he began hearing concerning stories over the few AM stations still broadcasting. It seemed the military roundups were aimed at eliminating remaining survivors, not supporting them in encampments. To destroy any chance of the virus spreading. Miles didn't want to take the chance of dying before he found Alice, so he abandoned his home in Seattle before the military could find him and set up a shelter on a remote hillside.

The shelter was difficult to reach by design. The fact that it was hard to reach, Miles figured, would also make it hard to find. Before that day, the location had never been a problem. In fact, Miles only left his shelter about once a week for supplies due to his understanding and implementation of rations and fasting.

Miles stood in the mud and examined his surroundings as best he could. The only sense he could rely on was his hearing, but even that was challenging with the pouring rain bouncing off the heavy limbs of the trees. He closed his eyes and listened carefully, taking into account the whistling stream, migration of big game, and plastic.

Plastic?

Miles's eyes shot open. He glanced up at the trees overhead to see if he could pinpoint where the sound was coming from. He looked left, then right. And then he saw it: a deer blind wedged between two Douglas firs. And a large one at that, big enough to lay down in. Its material, similar to an umbrella, reverberated the sound of every drop of rain that hit it. Though Miles had learned not to overexert himself unless absolutely necessary, he knew if he were to survive the night, he'd need to climb that tree.

Miles's swollen feet called out to him from inside his leather work boots, his toes still sore from when he crashed his foot into the fallen tree running from Mama Bear. He inhaled deeply and searched his mind for alternatives. Finding none, Miles flipped his muddy hood over his head and started climbing. Left foot, right foot, skipping branches when he could, rain pelting his face all the while. He glanced at the ground to see how high up he had climbed, careful not to let his glasses slip from his face. It looked like eight feet at least, but he could hardly tell through the darkness. All he knew was that he could touch the base of the stand with his hand when he reached upward.

Just a few more feet.

A strike of lightning lit the sky above, sending a flash of luminance to light his way. A roar of thunder followed. Amid the bright light, Miles spotted the half ladder that hung from the stand itself.

Suddenly, his foot gave way, slipping from a damp limb. Miles grabbed hold of the half ladder and pulled with all his might, using the last of his energy to hoist himself up and into the shelter. He sat on his knees, trying his best to catch his breath, and zipped the lining of the door closed against the rain.

Miles tore off his backpack and reached into one of its many side pockets for his Zippo lighter. Nothing scared Miles more than the unknown. And not knowing if he was truly alone in the shelter made him only move faster. When he finally pressed his thumb to the flint wheel, the flame proved that he was, in fact, safe at last.

———

THE NEXT MORNING came three hours later than usual for Miles, but he was unbothered given that he felt somewhat better than he had the past few mornings waking up in the cabin. Maybe it was the sweet lullaby of mother nature's tears that did it, or maybe it was the come down from the adrenaline-induced high he'd experienced before he'd passed out from pure exhaustion. Whatever it was, he felt pretty good, and it was definitely time to get moving.

It was 10 A.M., and the sun was high in the sky. Miles rolled up the sleeves of his moss-green pullover hoodie, then fished out a gallon of water from his bag and took a sip. The fresh water did wonders for quenching his thirst and did even more for his skin when he poured a little in his hand and rubbed his face clean of the dried mud and dirt from the previous night. Though he wanted to do much more, he had neither the time nor the luxury.

I'll never take another shower for granted as long as I live?

It had been months since Miles had done anything remotely close to his old daily routine. The cabin had no running water and no electricity, so he took his chances in town at hotels and schools every now and then, hoping he wouldn't get attacked while vulnerable.

Miles zipped up his backpack, making sure every strap was snug, then unzipped the shelter door and scanned the surrounding area for any potential danger that might come sprinting toward him as soon as he'd touch ground. Satisfied that there were no apparent threats nearby, he spun around and poked his foot out to see if he could touch a branch strong enough to hold his body weight. Holding the ladder with one hand, he gingerly released more and more of his weight down onto the limb below.

The limb snapped. Miles swung from the ladder, smacked the trunk of the tree, and crashed to the ground with a heavy thud. He let out a shriek of pain.

His arm went limp. He couldn't move it. He had never experienced such pain before. Certainly, a ten-foot drop would've done some damage. Could he have broken his arm? Miles tried to move but to no avail.

If only I had landed on my back, maybe my bag would've taken most of the impact.

Miles lay motionless on the forest floor face first in the mud, in pure agony, surrounded by the dead leaves from the previous autumn. He heard a rustling in the distance: an animal moving among the brush. Had the bear come back to seek vengeance? Had a Silent One heard him fall and come to dine on his flesh? He didn't want to know, either way, so he closed his eyes and accepted his fate as the sound crept closer.

When the creature was close enough that Miles could hear its breath, he felt a soft tickling sensation at his fingertips.

In a jolting response, he rolled to his side and found a German Shepherd licking his hand. Its tan and black fur immediately filled Miles with a calm he hadn't felt in a long time. The bright red collar with a golden medallion hanging from it made things crystal clear: this dog was a sign from God.

She's alive! Alice is alive!

Sgt. Peppers, Alice's dog, stood right in front of him.

Am I dreaming? Did I die? Miles quickly tried to sit up using both arms, but another sharp pain struck him. He gritted his teeth until the worst of it subsided, but it lasted long enough to allow him to pinpoint where exactly the pain was coming from. It was his left shoulder. He could move his hand and forearm, but not his shoulder. He had dislocated it.

Miles quickly rolled back over to his front and got to his knees with the help of his other hand. But as soon as he did, a few footsteps slithered behind him, followed by the click of a cocking weapon.

Miles quickly threw his right hand up. "Don't shoot! I'm unarmed." He lied. His baseball bat was strapped to the side of his backpack as plain as day. His heart began to race. He surely could've used a Xanax right about now, but his bottle of medication was back at the cabin. He was down to taking one pill every other day because he only had six left. And if he didn't find some soon, he'd surely die of a panic attack from all the stress he was under.

But at least Sgt. Peppers was alive, which meant Alice had to be alive. At least, Miles hoped that's what it meant. But if that were the case, then shouldn't it be Alice behind him? Why wasn't she saying anything? Miles realized he looked quite different now from when they last saw each other, with his long muddy hair in a ponytail and his dirty, raggedy clothes still damp from the night before. But still, he believed Alice definitely would've noticed his rather unique high-pitched voice, not to mention the fact that Sgt. Peppers didn't attack him.

"Please don't shoot me," Miles pled, his body still quivering in fear that one wrong move could put an end to his life. "I'm just tryna get home."

Sgt. Peppers barked. Miles listened closely to the person holding him at gunpoint shush the dog. *That doesn't sound like Alice.*

Slowly turning to see who had him in check, Miles found a six-foot-five, broad-shouldered, Black man where he hoped to see Alice standing. The man's jaw looked square from what Miles could make out under his five o'clock shadow, and his massive, chiseled, body took the shape of an inverted triangle. The dog tags around his neck implied he had served in the military at some point before the *Great Reset.*

"How'd you get Sgt. Peppers?" Miles asked him. He

hoped he made the right decision in choosing not to remain silent.

"How do you know Sgt. P?" the man said, answering Miles's question with another. His voice was deep and mellow-toned.

Miles didn't respond. Staring deep into the man's hazel eyes, he searched for an ounce of remorse—of shame for a past wrong the man had committed. *Did he murder Alice; or were they allies?*

"He's my girlfriend's dog," Miles finally answered. "I've been looking for her since... all this."

The man grew wide-eyed as Miles spoke. He quickly lowered his weapon as two other people, dressed in matching cement-grey cargo pants, black leather boots, and thermal tops, approached from behind. He turned to them.

"I've found another straggler," the burly man said. "A *live* one at that."

7

"What's your name, kid?" the light-brown-skinned woman of the group said, sliding the assault rifle behind her shoulder.

The man grabbed Miles from under his good shoulder and hoisted him up off the ground. "Miles. Miles Winstead."

"Nice to meet you, Miles, I'm Rebecca Farsi," the woman said. "You can call me Beck for short." She motioned to her two partners. "This is Ryan Lin, and the man holding you up is Victor White."

"Call me Vic," Victor said, lugging Miles over to the fallen log so Beck could assess his shoulder. He flashed Miles a wide smile that would have put him at ease if he hadn't just been holding a gun to Miles's head.

Beck knelt down in front of Miles. "You all alone out here?"

Miles didn't answer.

"Said he's just trying to get back home," Vic said.

"Home?" Beck questioned. "You seem pretty far away from any place a person might call a home, wouldn't you say?"

That's the point. Miles readjusted himself on the log, remaining mute.

Checking the perimeter, Ryan said, "Well, I guess us running into him was a good thing then. It looks like he needs some assistance."

"That right?" Beck examined Miles's shoulder. "Do you need help?"

"No." Miles lied. He didn't want to show any signs of weakness in front of three strangers who could just be fishing for information, hoping to rob him assuming he knew more than he led on about something of value. Yet he knew he could no longer fend for himself the way his shoulder was, making him hunch over, leaning to one side as if he were an old man.

Beck placed her duffle bag down on the tree and fished out a bottle of oxycodone. "Take this." She handed him a pill. "We're not going to harm you. You just so happened to be under our deer blind, that's all." She peered up, finding the zipper of the entrance flapping in the gentle breeze. "Looks like you took a pretty nasty fall."

"Yeah, I did," Miles said. "No biggie. Shit happens."

Beck stood and exchanged glances with Vic and Ryan. Then she looked back at Miles. "You probably think we're just like everyone else out here. Dangerous. Searching for something. I get it. You're smart to be cautious, and hell, if I were you, I'd be the same way. But we're different, Miles, and that's the truth. We have a place. A safe place for survivors. For people just like you. We even have a doctor there who can reset your shoulder."

Miles held off on taking the medication. "I can't go. There are things at my cabin I need."

"It's okay," Vic said. "We can come back and pick up your stuff tomorrow. You're in no shape to carry anything right now."

Vic was right, Miles's shoulder was on fire. His chest tightened. "I can't... I just can't."

"But don't you want to see your girlfriend?" Ryan asked, then motioned to Sgt. Peppers. "You said he was your girlfriend's dog, right?"

Of course, Miles wanted that. More than anything else on Earth. Yet, an uneasy feeling dwelled in the pit of his stomach. There was a long pause while he considered the question carefully.

Could they be telling the truth? Could Alice be waiting for me back at this . . . place?

If they really had a doctor, Miles could get relief for his shoulder. And Miles was in dire need of relief. The oxycodone Beck had handed him burned in his palm. But was it truly oxycodone? *If it is, could that mean they have access to Xanax as well?*

He wondered whether he really had a choice at all. If they insisted that he go with them, it was three against one, and Miles knew he stood no chance against them. They had military-grade weapons, and he had nothing. Just a baseball bat with screws drilled into the end cap clipped to his back-pack. Even if they agreed to let him go, they could follow him back to the cabin; then what would stop them from robbing him of all his belongings and putting a bullet in his head? He shuddered at the thought.

Then an idea arose: *I know exactly how to find out if they're lying.*

His heart was racing now, and he imagined all three of them could hear how loud it was pounding from within his bird-chest. The pressure had built up so much that he couldn't hold it in anymore. "You guys say I'll find my girl-friend at this place where you live. But you never mentioned her name," he pointed out. "What is it?" He had a stern look on his face.

Ryan scoffed as he took a seat on the log next to Miles. Sgt. Peppers poked his nose at his hand, begging to be pet. "Your girlfriend's the one with red hair, right?" he began. "Sort of petite with freckles, goes by Alice? Oh, and you can't forget that smile. It's brighter than a lighthouse!"

Miles's mouth slowly gaped as a mountain of doubt lifted from his shoulders.

"I guess you guys do know her," Miles conceded. "But where is this *place* you mentioned? I've covered a lot of ground over the last few months and haven't found anything remotely close to a thriving community."

"Oh, you never would've found us," Beck explained, "because we're not above ground; we're under it."

"Excuse me?" Miles assumed he hadn't heard correctly.

"In fact, that's what we call it: *The Underground*," Vic

said. "The original Pioneer Square of the 1800s. But we'll give you the full history lesson when we get back. We're burning way too much daylight right now."

Of the three, Vic definitely looked like the person who ran the show, though he didn't talk like it. If anything he acted more like a gentle giant, like Sloth from *The Goonies*. As for Beck, even if she wasn't exactly calling the shots, she played the perfect leader. Her hourglass-shaped body, blemish-free light-brown skin, and facial features resembling that of Middle Eastern descent brought on a daring allure. She seemed to be the one in command compared to the short, stocky Asian man who was just as jacked as Victor, who went by Ryan. Miles found they had their own unique qualities from the few minutes of conversation with them: Vic being the brute force behind the group, Ryan the five-star negotiator, and Beck the brains.

Having made his decision, Miles threw back the oxycodone and washed it down with some water. "I'm ready," he said. "Let's go."

Vic helped Miles up from the log, and the pair followed after Beck and Ryan as they crossed back over the stream. Before long they arrived at their destination: a charcoal-grey Ford F-450 crew cab parked behind a few bushes in a ditch right next to the highway off-ramp.

———

STARING out the window of the Ford, Miles admired the quiet atmosphere of the city he had grown to ignore: the great bucks and does grazing in the parking lot of the Pavilion Mall, the large flocks of birds bathing in huge rain tubs formed in empty trash dumpsters, the morning glories and honeysuckles that lined a majority of the elementary schoolyard chain-linked fences. The bright and colorful scenery brought on a sense of calm that was quickly diminished once the truck passed through the second set of twenty-foot-tall, concrete-walled barriers the National Guard had put up within the early weeks of the outbreak.

"Here we are," Beck said, turning off the music coming from a CD she had inserted. "Back in the heart of the city."

"I can't believe I forgot how beautiful this place is," Miles said, gazing at the overgrown terrain.

Having spent most of the *Great Reset* on foot in wooded areas, focused exclusively on survival, he had forgotten all about the city and its beauty.

"Yep, ground zero, or what remains of it," Vic said.

"And now there's nothing left but empty buildings and scrap metal," Ryan said, peering out the side window at the charred, abandoned vehicles spread about. "It's a shame what humans have done to this planet."

Miles tried to look at the environment in the same way as Ryan. He started to see it: buildings trashed, their bricks charred from the fires, and windows broken out. Some buildings had even collapsed. There was nothing left. Only ruins.

The truck maneuvered through a sea of abandoned vehicles.

"The efforts by our governor to quarantine the city—

starting here—made no difference." Beck turned left at the light. "The poison was in our food, and with the way our infrastructure was set up, our fall was inevitable. Luckily, there's only one way to contract the virus now..."

"By getting bit," Vic finished.

Miles tried to follow the thread of conversation, but it was hard not to dwell on the idea that soon, maybe very soon, he would finally see Alice again. Hug her. Kiss her. Ask where she's been. Miles wanted nothing more than to see a familiar face, to be close to someone who he had been close to long before the world collapsed.

Beck brought the truck to a stop at an intersection, and all three members of the team began to scan the area to make sure no one was watching them. Miles joined them as they craned their heads in every direction, looking for any signs of life and movement. Not a peep came from anywhere except the chugging exhaust pipe of the diesel vehicle they rode in. Passing a large fueling tractor trailer parked nearby, they turned left into the AMB parking garage and parked on the top level. Vic reached into Beck's backpack that sat between his legs and fished out a walkie-talkie. He turned it on and handed it to her.

"Come in, Boyd, I repeat, come in," Beck said, speaking into the handheld device. "Where's my eye in the sky?"

"At your six," the voice answered seconds later.

Beck smiled at Vic. "Beautiful. Do we have the all clear?" Her eyes wandered as she waited for a reply from the man on the other end.

"All clear."

"Thanks. Over and out." Beck returned the walkie-talkie to Vic, then peered back at Miles. "You know how to shoot a gun, right? Because you won't be swinging that bat anytime soon." She tossed Miles the Beretta 92 that was strapped to her hip before he even answered. "Safety's on the left."

Miles froze. He felt his heart skip a beat, then restart at an alarming rate. He immediately focused on counting in his head: *One, two, three, breathe. One, two, three, breathe. One, two, three...* Despite the calming rhythm, his heart rate didn't decrease.

The others opened their doors and got out of the Ford, but Miles stayed put. Ryan was the first to notice. "What's wrong?"

"I don't like guns," Miles managed to spit out between panicked breaths, trying his best to hand the weapon back to Beck without moving his left shoulder.

"You don't *like* guns?" Vic questioned. "How the *hell* have you been able to survive this long?"

"By staying hidden mostly," Miles answered, his nerves settling a little more after Beck retrieved the weapon from his hand.

They all stared at him in utter amazement. It wasn't necessarily the fact that he didn't like guns that shocked them, but rather that he was standing in front of them telling them so.

Miles opened his door and slid out of the truck, followed by Sgt. Peppers. When he turned and closed the door, something caught his eye. It was Smith Tower—once the tallest building in Seattle. He tried to take a moment to bask in its elegance, but he found it difficult with the way its many windows reflected the beaming sun. He held his right hand up over his eyes, trying to block some of the reflection, but it didn't help.

"You coming?" Ryan asked.

Miles quickly caught up with the team as they walked down the stairs, out of the parking garage, and across the street. There, Beck inserted a key into a heavily reinforced metal door, opened it just enough to let the team through, and then closed it quickly behind them. Miles followed them down a stairwell and through a series of corridors and misshapen passageways, at the end of which he found a cramped open space holding a few dozen people.

Is this it? It can't be.

Exposed brick—worn and decrepit looking—lined the walls, old wooden tables and chairs stood about, and dust covered most everything. The place looked like it hadn't been touched in decades—a straight-up ghost town.

Luckily, they kept walking, and as they traveled further into the catacombs of the lost city, everything came to light. The team led Miles into a dimly lit cellar, then up a long flight of stairs and into a building on one of the main streets of Seattle.

What he saw had him in awe. Besides the barricaded doors and boarded-up windows, the place looked the same as it had before the *Great Reset* like it hadn't been affected whatsoever.

"Here it is," Vic said, pointing out a giant hall where many people stood. "The Underground."

"We have close to a hundred people living here," Ryan said, closing the door to the stairwell. "Husbands, wives, children... even animals."

Miles spotted another furry mutt and a cat roaming around.

"This place is your one-stop shop for anything and everything survival." Beck led Miles down a hall, passing by many rooms that had different activities in motion. "We offer basic survival skills from gun training to cooking, self-defense, communications, and even sustainable farming. Pretty much everything."

The sight stunned Miles. He had never witnessed such chemistry between people before. An oasis of such size. Each of them knew exactly what part they played and did it well. Miles couldn't help but wonder what kind of leadership it took to form a community like The Underground.

8

Lost in a trance, Miles admired the many new faces he'd soon meet. People of all ages and ethnicities—men, women, some seeming to express no gender at all—nearly all of them wearing the exact same clothing as the people who had found him in the woods.

While Miles was gawking at the myriad of people, a burly man approached him. "Do you have any weapons?" he asked. The man's gruff voice scared Miles. Tattoos of skulls and other beastly images began at the man's neck and came together to form a sleeve that ran down his right arm.

"Just a baseball bat." Miles's voice cracked, but he was happy enough just to have been able to get any sound out at all in that particular moment.

"Cedric, meet Miles," Beck said, pulling the baseball bat from Miles's bag and showing Cedric. Then she turned to Miles. "We house all our weapons in the armory. Follow me."

Miles followed Beck to a door that read ARMORY. Through it they went, followed by Vic and Ryan. The room had a few fold-up tables spread about. Modular display racks were bolted to the wall above each table, upon which hung a plethora of military-grade assault rifles, submachine guns, and pistols. It looked like a gun store, only one in which people could pick out any weapon they wanted and check it out, like a book in a library.

"You're lucky we found you," Ryan said. "Not many of the other groups are as generous as us."

"Groups?" Miles questioned, watching Beck place her duffle bag on a table and slide it over to the gentleman who was supervising the cache.

"Yeah, groups." Vic threw down his duffle bag next to Beck's. "We're just a few of the many talented shots within the compound."

"Whatever you need to tell yourself," the man behind the counter said.

"Oh shut it, Sal," Vic shot back. "You're just jealous 'cause I'm a better shot than you." Turning back to Miles, he continued. "Anyway, there are five expedition groups. We're trained to go out in search of food, supplies, and water. Each group rotates shifts every week. No one else leaves the compound."

"Vic's right by the way," Ryan chimed in. "The other groups probably would've taken off as soon as you said you didn't need help."

Sal inspected Beck's duffle bag to see what the group had collected on their excursion. "Great, more explosives.

Ain't no one gonna bother us now." He handed the bag to his partner to put away, then inspected Vic's bag. "And some body wash, too. You guys sure hit it big today."

Beck, Vic, and Ryan unloaded their weapons and placed them on a table, followed by Miles's bat. "We've got an extra weapon for you to check in today," Beck said.

Sal grabbed the baseball bat and chuckled. "I remember when I had one of these. Sure is a classic." He looked at Beck, handing the bat off. "You guys score us any dinner?"

"Unfortunately, no. That plan was put on hold once we found him." She motioned to Miles. "But it's alright, though. We'll shoot some tomorrow." She headed for the door, Vic and Ryan following.

The more Miles learned, the more he was astonished at how the Underground was run. It was as if every detail had been meticulously designed, from the armory to the security, the education system, and even the location. It was the perfect example of hiding in plain sight.

"It's amazing, isn't it?" Ryan asked, grabbing Miles's good shoulder.

"Ahh, wonderful!" a woman said, slowly approaching the group. "You guys found another survivor." She looked at Miles. "Welcome, to the Underground. I'm one of the founding members." She extended a hand. "Name's Serenity. What's yours?"

"I'm Miles." He shook her hand and bit his lip to keep himself from asking about Alice. Everyone was being so nice; he didn't want to appear to be impatient, especially not in front of someone who clearly had some sort of leadership role in this fascinating place called the Underground.

Serenity examined his shoulder. "You look pretty banged up. Dr. Raines should be able to fix that for you." She looked at Ryan then, and though it was clear she was giving him an order, her words were gentle: "I think she's in her office."

Ryan nodded before leading Miles down the hall to a door with a sign that read INFIRMARY. The door had been left ajar, so Ryan knocked softly and then opened it without awaiting a response. Inside was an elderly woman sitting at a wooden desk. She was deep in a book of some sort—whether a medical book of some kind or a fiction novel, Miles couldn't tell. The room was set up like a small doctor's office: a few body diagrams pinned to the walls, a computer for storing patient data, a glass cabinet filled with a variety of medications, and a cooler for storing cold chain products such as blood used for transfusions.

"Dr. Raines?" Ryan said. "We've got another one for you. His name is Miles."

"Wonderful!" she said, placing a bookmark inside whatever book she was reading and jumping out of her chair to begin working on her new patient.

Dr. Raines was round and much shorter than Miles, with tree-barked wrinkles around her eyes. She grabbed Miles's arm and pulled him toward the treatment table so she could assess his wounds.

Geez!

Miles hadn't expected a woman of Dr. Raines's age to have such a tight grip.

Ryan left as the doctor checked Miles's vitals, taking his blood pressure and checking his temperature, eyes, ears, and lungs. When that was finished, she gave him two options. "Do you want me to slip off your clothes from over your head; or cut them off?"

Miles knew slipping the hoodie over his head would cause more pain than he could possibly tolerate, so he chose the latter option. He didn't share with Dr. Raines how deeply that decision wounded him. Though his hoodie had seen better days, it had been a birthday gift in better times, and it was the last connection he had to his father.

Dr. Raines opened a drawer in her desk, pulled out a pair of old metal scissors, and split Miles's hoodie and T-shirt like the Red Sea. After slipping them off his shoulders, she inspected his bare torso and arms for bite marks, then examined the reddish-pink bruising around his shoulder.

"Have you been bit? Felt sick at all?" she asked.

Miles shook his head. "No."

"Diarrhea? Vomiting? Headaches?"

"No. Nothing. Sounds like you know what you're looking for."

Dr. Raines exhaled. "To be honest, we still probably don't know what all the symptoms are. We just cover the basics of any ol' cold and look for bite marks. If someone's experiencing symptoms but we don't find bite marks, we quarantine 'em for a week. Better safe than sorry."

"And if they turn?"

"Then we'll take care of them."

Take care of them?

"And if they don't turn?"

"If their symptoms improve over the course of the quarantine, they can join the rest of the community." The doctor put her hands about Miles's arm, preparing to reset his shoulder.

Miles's anxiety spiked with the sudden awareness that the pain he had endured so far wouldn't amount to anything compared to what he was about to feel. Dr. Raines handed him the scissors to hold and squeeze. His heart rate picked up.

One, two, three, breathe. One, two, three, breathe. Calm down Miles, it'll only take a—

That was as far as he got in his thoughts before she put her hands to work, realigning his dislocated shoulder with a brutal "POP!" Miles let out a shriek and dropped the scissors. They crashed to the floor. Despite the opioid he had taken, he still felt the throbbing sting of his shoulder snapping back into place.

On the upside, the deed had been done. Miles had been healed. Well, at least healed enough so he could stand up straight and use his arm again. His heart slowly returned to its usual rate as the doctor opened a walk-in closet.

"You handled that well," Dr. Raines said, digging through the mountain of clothing that hung on the racks. "For most people, it takes a few more tries to get it back in place."

"Lucky me I guess," Miles joked, rubbing at his shoulder.

"You look like a thirty-one. I have a shirt that'll fit, but I think we're fresh out of cargos in that size."

"Don't worry about the pants, mine are fine," he said, poking at the small tear on the left kneecap of his muddy blue jeans.

Dr. Raines pulled out a charcoal-black thermal from the closet and handed it to him. "I have to give it to you, a kid like you out there all alone. It takes a lot of courage."

Miles stared down at the shirt the Doctor had handed him, the threads of cotton soft and supple between his fingers. If only his parents could see how far he had come. If only he could've saved them.

"You think this'll ever end?" Miles asked. "If things will ever go back to normal?"

Dr. Raines grabbed his hand and held it tight. "I don't believe it will, Miles. But only time will tell." She turned away to close the closet door as she continued. "Even if we managed to stop people from turning, I don't think it would help. We've lost so many lives to the virus already. All we can do now is focus on survival." Silence fell, leaving the remaining sound to come from the flickering tube lights in the ceiling. "C'mon, let's get you cleaned up."

———

DR. RAINES LED Miles down the hall and into another room. It was empty. It had nothing but a few boxes filled with towels, washcloths, and body wash spread about the floor. She walked into the bathroom and turned on the water as Miles picked out some bathing materials. The old copper pipes creaked in the walls as the liquid traveled up deep in the ground below the building.

"You've got ten minutes," Dr. Raines said.

Miles nodded, watching her leave the room and head back to her office.

The smell of rotten eggs wafted up his nostrils. Though the slight sulfur smell was quite unpleasant, Miles cared more about whether the temperature of the water was to his liking. It had only been a week since he had taken a shower, but months since he had taken a hot one. Dare he hope?

When he stepped into the bathroom, closed the door, and ran his hand under the shower head, there it was: warm water at last. Miles couldn't remember the last time he had felt such warmth. Shedding his jeans and boxers, he stepped inside the curved ceramic tub. For ten minutes he stood there, suspended in oblivion, surrounded by hot steam as the water pelted his body, relieving it of all its impurities.

Through the showering rain, a gentle knock at the door caught his attention. "Miles?" a familiar voice shouted on the other end. The shower had only intensified his high, putting him in a blissful state, and causing him to lose track of time. He assumed Dr. Raines was on the other side informing him that his time was up. He quickly turned the water off, wrapped his lower half in a bath towel, and opened the door.

Two sets of eyes locked, and two mouths gaped in astonishment. Alice wrapped her arms around Miles's still-soaking wet body, almost tackling him to the tiled floors on which they stood.

"Oh my God, it is true," Alice said. "You're alive!" She squeezed him as tight as she could, innocently stealing the breath from his lungs. "I've missed you so much."

Miles tried to speak but was at a loss for words. He was in such bliss. They stood there holding each other for a long moment, frozen in time—their bodies pressed together; their hearts beating at the same rhythm.

Alice ran her hands down Miles's damp back, brushing against the split ends of his long hair. It had been so long since he had been touched, since they had touched. He'd almost forgotten what it felt like.

Alice laid her cheek against his bare chest. There was no greater feeling. "I'm so glad I found you," he whispered in her ear.

"Me, too," she said.

Dipping his head down, Miles pressed his mouth against hers. Her plump lips felt so good against his. She pulled him out into the empty room, leaving the steam to follow them out from the bathroom. As they tripped over each other's feet, Miles's bath towel loosened and fell from his hips. The air felt cold against his ass.

Alice grinned, stepping back to admire his slender frame. "You've lost weight. You still look good, though. But you could use a haircut." They both laughed.

Miles went in for another kiss as Alice shed her thermal. Giggling and laughing, they stumbled backward onto a pile of used bath towels. She unstrapped her cotton polka dot push-up bra and tossed it to the side. God, was she beautiful.

Her supple breasts were firm. Her nipples were even harder. She unbuttoned her pants. Sex wasn't on his mind, hadn't been for a while. Survival had taken its place. But her eagerness immediately awoke his own crushing need. But it wasn't just his need for Alice; it was a sudden release of all the emotions he'd been holding inside himself over all he had lost since the beginning of the *Great Reset*. The feeling was so deep, so overwhelming, that Miles felt engulfed by it.

As Alice slipped out of her cargos, revealing her matching panties, Miles experienced something he had only felt once before.

He could see it—not only on her body but in her eyes—Alice was aroused. But he wasn't. When Alice took note of his flaccid penis, she quickly withdrew her advances by sliding back into her pants. It was like his first time all over again.

"I'm sorry," he whispered, turning away in shame. "I don't know what's happening." He reached for his bath towel, stood, and rewrapped himself. "I think it's the painkillers I took earlier. I've never taken anything like that before."

Alice stood and put her bra back on. "It's okay, Miles. I can't say I'm not disappointed, but I know it's not your fault. It happens. We're both in shock. We can work up to it. Once I found out you were here, I couldn't wait. I had to come see for myself. I had to feel you again. So if anything it's my—"

"Don't say it! It's not your fault." Miles stepped into his

old boxers and jeans and tossed his towel onto the dirty pile.

"But it is," she shot back, sliding her thermal over her head.

Miles could sense the regret in her tone. Trying to have sex with him within an hour of his arrival at the compound wasn't a smart move.

After they finished getting dressed, Alice led Miles down the hall and onto an elevator. The compound was an office building that had been converted to residential on a few floors. It was old, but it met the needs of the many people who stayed there: clean, running water, electricity, and security.

"How have you been, Alice?" Miles asked as they waited for the elevator to arrive.

"I'm better now that you're here."

"No, seriously. How have you been holding up during all this?" He reached for her hand.

She bowed her head. "I... I don't know how to answer that, Miles. So much has happened the past six months that it still hasn't hit me yet."

He exhaled. *Maybe I shouldn't pressure her.* "Well, at least tell me this: where have you been all this time? I looked for you at your house, and you weren't there."

The elevator doors opened, and Alice answered. "After the outbreak, I crashed at my uncle's outside of town."

"Outside of town?" Miles questioned.

Alice *mhmm'd.*

"He was long gone when I got there, but he still had food and supplies, so I stayed."

They trekked down the hallway and into a large room. Inside were five rows of five single beds, all with off-white matching linens and sheets. They were differentiated only by the personal belongings laid atop each one: stuffed animals, kid's drawings, family heirlooms, many of them surely cherished remembrances of loved ones taken by the virus.

Miles smiled inwardly when he remembered what Alice had managed to hold on to; Sgt. Peppers.

"How'd you—"

"Miles, there'll be time for us to talk about all that," Alice interrupted. "Right now, let me finish showing you around, okay?"

Miles nodded. "Is this where I'm sleeping?"

Alice turned to him. "Unfortunately, not. You're probably on the fifth floor. That's where all the new arrivals go. But Serenity will let you know for sure once it gets closer to lights out. In the meantime, follow me."

Assuming there'd be many more rooms like the one in which they were currently standing, Miles was compelled to protest. He didn't want to say no to her, especially after accidentally rejecting her advances earlier, but his stomach was growling so loudly he was surprised she hadn't heard it yet.

"You think we could start with the kitchen or cafeteria or whatever?" Miles suggested, rubbing at his stomach. "'Cause I'm starving."

Alice cracked a smile. "Breakfast was served at eight o'clock so you missed out on that, but you're in luck. Lunch is about to get started."

9

Down the hall from the common area was a large dining room, perhaps once a venue space for weddings and conferences in happier times, filled with fold-up tables and metal chairs. As they walked in, Miles spotted Beck, Vic, and Ryan sitting at a table in the corner, with bowls, and utensils in hand.

"Thanks for bringing Miles back safely, guys," Alice said to all three when both of them joined the group. "I didn't know if I'd ever find him."

"*Please*," Ryan said. "After all the stuff you've done for us, we definitely owe you."

Done for us?

"But we can't take all the credit though," Vic said. "If it weren't for Sgt. P, I would've put a bullet in his head."

Miles shuddered as Vic let out a quick chuckle.

Beck backhanded Vic's shoulder. "Lay off the kid, man.

Lord knows what he's been through. Give him some time to settle in before you start joking around like that."

Vic shrugged. "What? It's true. You know I don't lie." He glanced over at Miles, who was by now visibly disturbed, then turned back to Beck. "Eh, maybe you're right. I guess I went too far."

"How about we get off the subject of killing people and move toward something positive," Alice suggested. "*Like,* guessing what we're having for dinner tonight since you guys didn't score any bucks."

"How about this," Miles suggested, nudging his glasses up on the bridge of his nose. "I've got tons of questions about this place: what it is, how it was developed. How you guys hide in plain sight."

Two people wheeled in a giant deep-well pot on a serving cart and stopped in the middle of the room. The savory aroma of thyme and the spice of cayenne danced on Miles's tongue.

"We'll answer all of your questions, but first, let's eat!" Ryan said, rising from his seat and heading toward the cart.

One of the people who had rolled the cart into the room marched toward the doorway to the hall and pressed a button on the wall three times. Three bells rang out over the building's intercom system, apparently notifying the community that lunch had officially begun.

At first, only a few people trickled in after the bell was rung, but a minute later they were flooding in like a dam failure. They all stood and rushed over to the pot of creamy potato soup, getting their bowls filled to the brim and receiving a piece of cornbread to go along with it. The five quickly returned to their seats and began eating.

Miles slurped the scorching soup from his spoon. "So how long have you guys been here? This place I mean?"

"I've been here three months," Beck answered first. "Three months and eight days to be exact. I came across this place after my group got ambushed by some Crazies."

"Crazies?" Miles questioned.

He had never heard that word used by anyone he had met upon his travels during the apocalypse.

"The cannibals, in layman's terms," Beck continued. "We call 'em Crazies around here, now that the world is... well, you know. But like I was saying, I was the only survivor of my group, and I was in pretty bad shape when I found this place. If it weren't for the doc patching me up, I don't know if I'd still be alive today."

"Sounds like you've been through a lot."

"She has," Ryan said, taking a bite of his cornbread. "She had taken a pretty bad fall just like you. Had two broken ribs and a bullet to the stomach." He glanced at Beck. "She's definitely a tough cookie."

Beck smiled at Ryan, smiling in a way that made Miles wonder if there might be more to their relationship than meets the eye.

"I've seen Dr. Raines heal a lot of people, Miles," Alice said, resting her hand on his thigh.

"Serenity, the doc, and I are the only remaining founding members of the Underground," Ryan said. "Unfortunately, the others are no longer with us."

"You've been here since the beginning?" Miles was surprised by this revelation. If he had been told that one of his three rescuers was a founding member, he'd have guessed Ryan last.

"Yep," Ryan admitted.

"How did you guys stockpile all the food, medical supplies—all those weapons?"

"In a way, we were able to get those things with the help of Alice and Boyd," Ryan said, scooping the last of his bowl clean with his spoon.

Boyd? Miles had heard that name before, but only once. It was when Beck had said it over the walkie-talkie when they first arrived. "Who's Boyd?"

"Boyd was the first outsider to join our community," Ryan answered.

"Your girlfriend here being the second," Vic added.

"With their help and understanding of renewable energy, we were able to set up solar panels on the roof to power what we needed for this place," Ryan said.

"And with electricity came communication," Beck added, pushing her empty bowl to the side. "Before the collapse, Boyd owned a pawn shop not too far from here. Most of the stuff got looted during the riots early on, but he kept a multi-band radio locked in his desk. We were able to use it to get in contact with the naval base over in Kitsap."

Miles leaned in so as not to miss a word of Beck's story, but faint whispers of different conversations from other tables permeated the room, trying their best to distract him.

"By that time, our community had grown to about

thirty-five people," Beck continued. "We managed to talk the base into shipping some food, supplies, and ammunition to us along with a few soldiers, and now here we are."

"And that's how I wound up in this *wonderful* place," Vic joked. He lifted his bowl and threw back the rest of his soup.

Beck rolled her eyes. "You've had multiple chances to return to base, Vic. You just can't get enough of us, and you can't bear the thought of leaving."

Vic scoffed. "Whatever."

Ryan refocused the conversation. "Now we've grown to eighty-seven people, so we've got enough manpower to hunt for game, manage crops, and search whatever places are still standing for things like canned and dried goods. So we're officially self-sustaining—pretty much."

Miles turned to Alice. "So this is where you've been hiding all this time? For the first month, I'd go to your house every day, but you weren't there. No one was. I even went to the school to look for you. But as things got worse, I couldn't stay at home anymore, so I went into hiding."

Alice placed her hand over his, giving it a loving grip. "As soon as the video of that man who came back to life aired online, my parents packed as much as they could and headed to the airport. Highway 5 was at a standstill. It was disastrous. After an hour of waiting, people got impatient and went on foot, which only made traffic worse. And like many others, my parents followed, dragging me with them. We ended up getting separated once we got to the airport. But by that time, the National Guard had set up small camps within the building, quarantining some and separating others. I haven't spoken to my parents since."

Spotting tears bubbling in her eyes, Miles placed his other hand atop hers and squeezed tightly. *I guess that explains where she's been, and how she's been.*

"I don't even know if they're still alive," she confided through the tears pouring down her cheeks.

The table fell silent. Miles had more questions, but now was not the time to ask. The group slowly stood and left, allowing Miles to gather Alice in a warm hug as they shared a moment of solace.

10

As hours passed and the day turned to night, the sun fell behind the mountains, cloaking the streets in darkness. Since the power had been cut to the city, the streetlamps were dead. A full moon provided the only light to the block below.

Miles had spent the last three hours lying in a bed, thinking about his parents. He couldn't sleep. Staring up at the unfinished ceiling—at the air duct tubing and support beams that held the floor above—he mulled over what he had done, what he didn't do, and what he could've done to save his parents. A tear trickled down his cheek, landing on his pillow.

I wish you guys were still here.

Then he thought about what tasks he'd be given the following morning that would solidify his contribution to the compound. *Hopefully, they don't make me go back out there. I don't think I can do it anymore.* He felt his heart rate begin to rise. To calm it, he pictured Alice—her bright smile and elegant glow.

Miles was in awe of the work Alice had done to establish the Underground. He'd been astonished when she showed him the large garden of vegetables and herbs she had set up on the roof, not to mention the rigged-up solar panels. They lead to the inverters and batteries just below the top floor, which in turn powered the entire building. Who would've thought she'd be of much help in a dying world? It gave him a glimmer of hope that maybe the two of them could survive the apocalypse and help play a major part in restarting life as they once knew it.

As his fellow survivors snored in their sleep, a spine-crippling noise penetrated his ears. It sounded like a door opening, its hinges in dire need of oil, followed by a loud slam. Miles shot up from the covers, his heart fluttering.

Relax. You're in a safe place now. Nothing can hurt you.

Miles looked around the room and saw that none of his bunkmates had moved. Believing he was the only one awake and alert—ready to attack an intruder—Miles snuck out of bed and grabbed his backpack. He dug his lighter from it, then left the room. With his Zippo in his right, his left hand traced along the walls as he slowly approached the stairwell.

He opened the door and quietly crept down the stairs to the first floor. On the main level, he stepped out of the stairwell into a shroud of pitch black. The large windows leading to the street were covered by reinforced plywood that didn't let in an ounce of moonlight. Not even his lighter provided enough illumination but only for the surrounding five feet around him. At least on the upper levels, the windows weren't covered by plywood, but rather black-clothed curtains that remained closed for a better part of the day.

Continuing to creep down the hall, trying his best not to hit something and knock it over, Miles spotted a man venturing down the hall. *Mmm, where's he going?* Miles watched as the man walked into a room, then traveled down a staircase that led to the cellar. He followed after him, staying as quiet as possible all while maintaining a safe distance between him and the man in an effort not to get caught.

The underground was pitch black. Maneuvering through the passageways would be damn near impossible if Miles lost sight of the man. Getting lost would be inevitable at that point. He'd just be another piece of furniture lurking around in the shadows.

After a few more minutes of tiptoeing, Miles heard the door to the outside unlock, open, then close again. *Shit.*

He rushed to the door, hoping it was still unlocked. It was. Putting out his lighter, he opened the door and snuck out onto the street. When Miles regained visual of the man, he noticed a sniper rifle strapped to his back.

Miles gasped. *How'd he get a gun?*

Continuing to follow the man across the courtyard, stumbling over sidewalks and debris left over from the early riots, Miles tripped and crashed onto the pavement. That's when the man turned and spotted him.

"Hey! What're you doing out here?" the man demanded in a faint raspy voice.

Miles froze, unable to stand, his nerves stopping him from moving an inch. The man approached Miles.

"I know you heard me." He lent a hand and hoisted Miles up off the ground.

Looking up, Miles found an elderly gentleman—a man he had not seen before during his tour of the place—staring down at him. The bald head of the Black man reflected the moonlight.

"Shouldn't you be in bed?" the man asked.

"In bed?" Miles questioned. "Shouldn't you be too?"

The man scoffed. "You must be new." He extended a hand. "I'm Boyd. Clarence Boyd."

Once Miles heard the name, it clicked. He was the man from the walkie-talkie. The man they talked about at dinner. He introduced himself. "If you don't mind me asking, what're you doing out here?"

"It's time for my shift," Boyd answered, continuing his walk to Smith Tower.

Shift? Then it dawned on him. Boyd was going to be the lookout up at the top of the tower, but why at midnight?

Approaching the miniature skyscraper, the stench of burning tobacco crept up Miles's nose. It came from a very large cigar, which was being smoked by a very short man Miles spotted leaning against the front doors of the building.

"You're late," the short man said to Boyd, exhaling a cloud of smoke and stepping aside to allow Boyd to pass.

"Blame the kid." He opened the door and entered the building, but Miles lingered behind. He smiled and introduced himself, extending his hand warmly to the short man.

But the man just stared at him, ash falling from his cigar. He flicked it from his hand and walked off, ignoring Miles's attempt at making friends.

Geez, what's his problem?

Miles rushed to catch up with Boyd, following him into the building. The place was ghost-quiet and as dark as the compound after lights out. Miles quickly pulled out his lighter once more and relit it. As he did, he spotted Boyd heading for the stairwell. They trekked up thirty-eight flights.

"What was that all about?" Miles asked.

"Oh, he's just sick of having the day shift is all," Boyd answered. "When you work from noon to midnight, you don't get to see many people."

"Ahh, I see. Makes sense."

By the time they reached the top flight, Miles was winded. Boyd didn't seem bothered by the walk at all. Maybe since he had traveled it so often, it no longer affected his lungs. Or maybe Miles's cardiovascular health lacked.

Boyd opened a door that read OBSERVATORY. They entered. Miles followed him inside and quickly glanced out the window down at AMB Parking Garage, spotting the back of the F-450. Then he examined the room in which he stood. He had never been to Smith Tower before, and his first impression wasn't exactly positive. Though it was dark like the compound, some candles lit the environment. Tables and chairs had been thrown about, some of them turned upside-down. Several bottles of whiskey were missing from the glass shelving above an island bar that scaled the ceiling. Some bottles had been shattered, leaving glass everywhere.

At least there aren't any bodies, thank God.

Quickly darting his eyes left and right, Miles realized something was missing.

"Boyd? Where are you?" he called out.

"Over here," Boyd answered, his voice coming from across the room followed by some crackling static.

Walking from around the bar, Miles saw it—two tables pushed together to make one large space for a whole host of radio equipment along with a battery bank. The battery bank was connected to something outside by way of a wire that led upward from it and out a window. Could it be powered in the same way as the compound: by solar? Possibly. The equipment looked similar to what Beck had described earlier during lunch, the stuff that helped them get in contact with Kitsap. But what was Boyd doing now?

"Do you know what this contraption is?" Boyd asked.

Miles examined the equipment, not knowing anything about it. He took a guess. "It's a multi-band radio?"

"You're half right."

Miles scratched the back of his head. "Well, Beck had mentioned something about it earlier today during lunch so I can't take all the credit."

He turned to Miles as he continued turning the dial knob, sweeping the channels in search of any sign of life. "This is what you call long-range communication on HF. With the right setup and a tall enough antenna you can talk to practically anyone in the world."

Suddenly, the system picked up something. Boyd's head shot back to the transceiver, realizing what channel he had just passed over. He turned the knob counterclockwise a tad until the faint voice became apparent. He reached for his headphones and plugged them in, then grabbed the microphone and spoke.

"Kitsap. This is Boyd calling in from Compound One. I repeat, this is Boyd calling in from Compound One."

Leaning forward, Miles put his head next to Boyd's to hear their conversation. Both Miles and Boyd shared a moment of silence as the person on the other end didn't respond. Boyd repeated himself once more.

Then, after a minute, the voice answered. "What's your status?"

"All good on this end. Got a new member of the compound with me tonight." Boyd smiled at Miles, then told him off the mic, "We haven't been able to reach any other bases besides Kitsap and USCG in Alameda, California. It doesn't seem like there's much life out there."

Miles rushed to grab a chair himself and slid it over next to Boyd. He handed Miles a second set of headphones to listen with.

"Wonderful," the man on the other end said. "Any luck making contact with anyone else?"

Boyd slid the microphone over to Miles, giving him a chance to experience the beauty of carrying on a conversation over HF. Miles glanced at Boyd in hesitation, afraid he might mess up or say the wrong thing.

"It's okay," Boyd whispered. "Tell him who you are, then answer him."

Nodding, Miles pushed the button to talk. "This is Miles, Boyd's copilot for the evening. From what I've been told, we haven't reached anyone other than you and the USCG. But that doesn't mean we won't. What about you guys?"

"Unfortunately, we haven't either," the man said. "We've only been able to remain in contact with other countries. Sadly, I don't think there's much left of this nation."

Miles's eyes grew wide. "This isn't global?"

"To answer your question, no. The U.S. has been the only country affected by the virus. Other nations have been reluctant to step foot onto American soil in fear the outbreak might leak into theirs. As of right now, South Korea has been the only one to help in our time of need."

Miles sighed. "I guess there's no hope for our future then, huh?"

"Hope?" the man shot back. "Hope is for the weak. It's faith you must have. Whether in the form of an antidote or military warfare, having faith is what's going to save us all. America will recover and rise again."

"Antidote?" Miles questioned. "Is there a cure that will save—"

"I can't disclose that information at this moment. But don't worry, we'll keep you posted. We'll broadcast a global message stating any recent findings and what we plan to do next if action is warranted. For now, I recommend you focus on the people around you. Enjoy every waking moment with them. Because as of right now, they're all we've got."

The transmission ended, and Miles set the microphone back down and turned to Boyd. "Did you hear that? A possible antidote."

Boyd nodded. "I did. This isn't the first time I've heard it mentioned, either. USCG wouldn't say much about it when I asked, but I believe they're the ones creating it."

Hope has been restored! I never thought I'd see her again, but here she is, alive and well. She even played a part in building this community called the Underground. I love how she's so free-spirited and willing to help others. I can't believe yesterday I contemplated killing myself. If I hadn't fallen out of that tree, Sgt. Peppers wouldn't have found me. And if I hadn't questioned them, I wouldn't have known for sure if she was alive. God, am I glad I found Alice.

But also I feel sad for her, 'cause she lost her parents, too. We don't know for sure if they're dead or not, but she hasn't seen or heard from them since the world went to shit. I hope they're still alive. Speaking of the world, it's only the United States that's been affected. If we could fly to another country we could escape. We could be free of all of this.

Sincerely, M.W.

11

iles awoke the following morning with a crook in his neck. His backpack couldn't beat a pillow, but it was better than nothing. Struggling to rise from the hard table—his back tight from the night's sleep—he swung his feet over the edge and stood. He spotted Boyd standing outside the window on the observation deck, scoping every inch of the city streets below with the use of lightweight field binoculars. Miles couldn't recall when he fell asleep. Maybe he was still asleep and dreaming. He didn't know for sure.

Walking over to the sliding glass door, Miles cautiously opened it and stepped out, taking deep breaths as he approached the railing. He gazed at the horizon line as the sun lifted from the depths of Elliot Bay and into the sky with grandeur. He had never witnessed the sunrise at such a high altitude before. In fact, he generally avoided high altitudes: Miles was afraid of heights. His anxiety is what did it. So he thought about Alice—his girlfriend was still alive and in one piece. That managed to calm his nerves a little.

"Morning," Miles said.

"Morning," Boyd said, still inspecting the perimeter. "It's beautiful isn't it?"

Miles leaned against the railing and took another deep breath. "It's outta this world."

He glanced over at Boyd and noticed he had been crying. He'd wondered why the man hadn't turned to him when he spoke, but now it made sense. He didn't want Miles to see his tears. But why was he crying?

His mother had taught him that assumptions offend people. Though Miles didn't want to offend Boyd, especially not after having known him for only a few hours, he felt he might be able to clear the air.

"I get the feeling I remind you of somebody," Miles said gently.

Boyd removed the binoculars from around his neck and placed them on the ground. He looked over at Miles in despair and sniffled, wiggling the caterpillar mustache above his lip. "His name's James. He's my son. He'd just turned thirty-one when the world went mad. You remind me of him. Smart, just like you. He's a doctor."

Turning away, Boyd took a deep breath and rubbed his eyes. Then clenched his fist. "James called me when the government declared a national state of emergency. Told me to stay home, but I didn't listen. I went out and did what I always do. But that was the last time I heard from him. If I'd just stayed in the damn house, maybe..."

Miles immediately understood what enormous weight hung over Boyd's shoulders. He was facing the unknown—that uncertain grief that Alice also faced. Could James still be alive? No one knew.

Boyd cleared the mucus in his throat. "The way you carried yourself last night when you were talking over the radio, reminded me of him so much. When he was a toddler, he and I would stay up late every night and listen to all the different transmissions we'd uncover." He wiped another tear from his eye. "To tell you the truth, I only set this stuff up so I could sweep the channels every night in hopes I'd hear his voice one more time."

Miles was taken aback by what Boyd had said. Yeah, his reasoning might've been a little selfish, but that's what you do for someone you love. Give a few minutes each day to exercise your faith and pay your respects in remembrance of what was lost.

"At this point, I don't even know if he's still alive."

As Boyd dwelled in the silence of his sorrows and grief, the walkie-talkie clipped to his brown leather belt beeped, followed by a crackle, then a familiar voice.

"Come in Boyd! We're heading out," Beck announced. "Gonna catch us some dinner for tonight."

Miles gasped, recognizing who it was. "Wait, let me see the walkie."

Boyd handed Miles the device.

"Hey Beck, it's Miles. What about my stuff we left behind yesterday? I can't be without it."

"Agghhh, I completely forgot. Do you truly need any of it?"

"Yes! My meds are there."

"What meds are you taking?"

"Xanax."

After Miles answered, silence followed. He assumed she was talking it over with Ryan and Vic. Then suddenly, the walkie-talkie crackled again.

"Alright, hurry down so we can get a move on."

Miles dashed toward the door, darting down the steps of the dimly lit staircase, his shoulder still tight from the previous day. He scurried through the decadently marbled lobby and out the front doors of Smith Tower to find them patiently waiting for him.

Everyone was dressed in the same gear they'd worn when he had encountered them the day prior: cement-grey cargo pants, black leather boots, thermals. Despite his matching charcoal-black thermal, he still stood out like a sore thumb in his old blue jeans and tan boots.

"I appreciate you guys for helping me out."

"We're only doing this because we said we'd take you to pick up your stuff," Beck said. "That's all. If you didn't need medication, then you'd be shit outta luck."

"I highly doubt he's going to want to join us on the hunt, Beck," Vic said, unlocking the F-450. "So it looks like we're making two trips today."

They all got in and buckled their seatbelts, then took off.

"Hey, where's Sgt. Peppers?" Miles asked.

"Right there," Ryan said, pointing ahead out the window.

Alice! What is she doing out here?

Pulling up next to Alice walking the dog, Beck stopped the truck and rolled down the window. "Wanna come?"

"Sure," Alice answered, noticing Miles in the backseat.

Ryan opened the back door and stepped out, allowing Alice to sit in the middle. Then he helped Sgt. Peppers into the bed of the truck.

"You sure you wanna tag along? We're just getting my stuff," Miles asked.

Alice got comfortable and buckled her seatbelt. "Sure, why not? I want to see where you've been hiding all this time."

Miles had only known Alice to be gentle and motherly, but that twenty-four-inch machete hanging from the strap on her back made him think about how much more there was to learn about her. A small fire was lit inside him. *The last six months of hell have turned her into a warrior. Or was she always a warrior, and I just never noticed?*

Still, Miles couldn't keep his protective instincts from bubbling to the surface. "I just don't want you to get hurt."

"*Please...* I can take care of myself, Miles."

Miles fell silent as the truck took off. He couldn't tell her the real reason he didn't want her to come. The way he had survived the last six months was—by his definition—cowardly, and he didn't want her to see that. He had promised her, the last day they saw each other, that he'd no longer allow his anxiety to control his life. But that had proved to be a lie. It still haunted him from day to day, preventing him from sleeping, eating, or even making basic decisions for his survival. Though he'd grown somewhat better at controlling his handicap, he still succumbed to it.

THE CITY WAS STILL WAKING. The streets echoed every bird chirp and mating call imaginable across many blocks as the smell of damp grass lingered. Peering out the windows of the vehicle, both Alice and Miles admired what ruins were left of the city as Beck cautiously maneuvered through the sea of abandoned vehicles scattered about the streets. As they drove north, in the emergency lane on the highway, they ended up back where they'd found Miles the previous day. Beck pulled the truck over.

"Keep going!" Miles said. Beck peered back at him through the rearview mirror with a puzzled look on her face. "I only took this route because I was on foot and didn't wanna run out of daylight. We can get there faster in the truck if you stick to the road. Keep going. I'll let you know when to turn."

Beck pressed her foot to the accelerator pedal and continued onward, receiving directions from Miles the rest of the way until they arrived at a small log cabin. It was situated down on a bend off a long dirt path behind a ruff of trees that had overgrown and covered the house from the main road.

"This place looks a mess, Miles," Beck said.

The wretched building—its interior and exterior decrepit—looked completely abandoned and in terrible shape. Its windows were boarded up, and a majority of the structure had been eaten away by termites and burrowed into by carpenter bees.

Beck turned off the truck. Miles was the first to step out, taking his time not to slip and fall in the gooey mud from the last day's rainfall. Nothing but the faint sound of rustling leaves and tree limbs in the morning breeze surrounded them. He inhaled deeply, taking in all of mother nature's earthly scents.

Serenity at last.

Inspecting the premises to make sure nothing had changed or been moved, Miles approached the building as the others got out of the truck. To his relief, nothing looked out of the ordinary. He approached the front door and pressed his ear against the boarded-up window to see if he could hear any movement inside. Nothing. Total silence.

Miles rested his hand on the doorknob, then glanced back at the rest of the group whispering, "Be ready, just in case."

Everyone's shoulders tensed as they drew their weapons and aimed at the door. The creaking hinges screamed as the door crept open. Streaks of light from the boarded windows barely lit the cabin. Miles quickly pulled out his Zippo, lit it, and snuck inside, hoping nothing was waiting for him. His heart was racing now. He tried his best to remain calm as he searched for a candle. Successfully avoiding tripping over the few boxes of supplies and the old mattress he'd left scattered on the floor, Miles located his box of candles right where he'd left them on the counter. He pulled one out and lit it, but as soon as the wick ignited, something jumped out at him, causing him to squeal and fall back onto the couch.

Sgt. Peppers stormed in at the sound of Miles's distress, and the others quickly followed after him, only to find a squirrel darting about who'd taken refuge in Miles's absence. Beck quickly pulled out her Beretta 92 and put the rodent in her sights.

"Don't shoot it!" Alice yelled, putting her hand atop the barrel of the weapon, urging Beck to lower it. "It's harmless. Leave it be. We're only here to pick up some stuff anyway, right?" Beck nodded as she re-holstered the weapon.

Miles gathered himself up from the couch as the others took a good look around now that the place was somewhat lit and the coast was clear. The cabin had been the perfect hiding place, not only with its secluded location but also with what it harbored inside: an old cast-iron wood stove, some cabinet space, and an outhouse. It was far from perfect, but it was enough to make do, especially with the old well-water hand pump right outside.

Miles quickly grabbed the few things he wanted to keep and stuffed them inside the suitcase he'd carried with him from home: the rest of his clothes, his toothbrush, a map, and, last but not least, his bottle of anxiety medication. The team quickly regrouped back at the truck and headed back down the mountain. As they drove away, Miles peered out the back window and watched as his private safe haven faded in the distance.

12

As they drove back down Highway 5, jamming along to one of Beck's CDs, she slammed on the brakes, bringing the truck to a quick stop in the middle of the free-way. Everyone looked at her in outrage.

"What the hell, Beck!" Vic exclaimed.

"Shut it!" she shot back, pointing out the window. "Look what's ahead of us."

Everyone brought their attention to the horde of the undead that blocked the highway in front of them. Though they could've simply plowed through them like a bowling ball, having no effect on the overall structure of the Ford, something didn't seem right. Why hadn't they seen the horde on their way to grab Miles's stuff?

Ryan turned the safety off on his gun. "Where'd they come from?"

"I didn't see them on our way up," Vic added.

Nudging the glasses up onto the bridge of his nose, the

scene came into focus. Miles spotted a setup. Tire spikes had been rolled out across the road behind the horde. And their hands were tied together with rope, forcing the group to stay together.

"I knew it!" Beck said.

Sgt. Peppers started barking at something behind them.

"Knew what?" Alice asked.

"Shit," Ryan uttered after spinning around to see what had alarmed the dog. "We've got company."

Miles reached for Alice's hand in worry as they both turned to find a huge military vehicle crawling out of the woods and onto the asphalt.

"Crazies!" Vic said.

In all his time of surviving alone in the apocalypse, Miles had never crossed paths with anyone remotely considered *crazy*. But when he saw some questionable figures step out of the heavy-duty vehicle, it sent a crippling shiver down his spine.

There were five of them: young and old, all sporting patent-leather *BDSM*-type apparel that was very revealing. And whatever skin wasn't concealed by the shiny black material was instead covered in blood and guts. Even their faces were covered. One guy had what looked like someone's lower intestines wrapped around his neck like a scarf.

But what scared Miles the most wasn't the intimidating-looking people, nor the heavy military-grade vehicle they rode in, but rather the tall, slender, yet robust woman that led the pack. Her hair was bright orange, short, and spiky. All and all, they looked like something straight out of a *Mad Max* movie. Miles swallowed the lump in his throat.

Beck shot back around and put the accelerator pedal to the floor, heading around the tire spikes, but as soon as the truck moved an inch, three more people stormed out of the trees on dirt bikes, pulling up onto the highway beside the horde. Guns were drawn and aimed at them from both directions. The only way out now was to fight.

"Safeties off," Beck said, unbuckling the clip on her holstered weapon. "It's gonna be a bloodbath."

She was the first to open her door. She swung her leather boots out over the cracked pavement and looked back in. "Follow my lead."

Vic and Ryan both nodded as they double-checked to see if their weapons were loaded and ready to fire.

Miles shuddered in his seat as the others stepped out. *It's either you or them. What's it gonna be?*

Miles's stomach churned like freshly made butter, his leg nervously tapping away as his pits seeped through his shirt. He couldn't get ahold of himself. Thinking back, he should've taken a pill before leaving the cabin. But who knew something life-threatening would arise on their way back to the compound?

Beck was the first to put her hands up as Vic and Ryan followed. "Don't shoot," she yelled, inching slowly toward the fiery-red-haired woman who led the pack.

"Don't move another inch," the woman shouted from afar.

Everyone froze, including Miles and Alice who were

inside the cab, their eyes peeking out just over the backseat. The woman's stance was menacing, but her voice was fairy-like: light and playful but with a splash of insanity.

"My colleagues will collect your weapons. And if you try anything, my love will light you up." She giggled, pointing out the hefty, muscular, shirtless man who occupied the turret atop the military vehicle.

"What do you want?" Beck gently asked.

"Just food. But you knew that already." The woman giggled again as three henchmen approached to confiscate their weapons.

Miles and Alice exchanged glances, but when they did, his door flew open, almost sending him falling into the hands of a blood-drenched weirdo. The man grabbed Miles. From the bed of the truck, Sgt. Peppers growled at the second man and nipped at him, almost stealing one of his fingers. Backing away, another came in and hit the dog on the snout with the butt of his machine gun. Sgt. Peppers yelped, then slowly retreated, rubbing his snout and whimpering in pain.

The man yanked Miles out of the seat by his right arm. Slapping at the back of the man's head and neck, Miles tried with all his might to escape, but it was of no use. Alice came next, dragged out of the truck like a naughty five-year-old who was about to get disciplined. Beck, Vic, and Ryan turned to find them squealing and squirming in fear, trying their best to break free from the henchmen's grasps.

"Let them go!" Beck shouted to the woman.

"Yeah, they're just kids!" Ryan added.

The dastardly woman cheered and clapped with glee. "Ohh, yay, kids... they will make a perfect spread for tonight." She laughed once more as a few others joined in.

"Look, just take us," Ryan said, lowering his hands. "Leave them." A few of the Crazies drew their weapons with haste, aiming them at his torso. "Okay, okay." He returned his hands to the air. "Let's work something out."

The woman playfully lifted her chin as if in careful deliberation. "What do you have in mind?" Then immediately added, in a slightly deeper voice, "No, that's not an option." It was like two people were speaking through one body like she had a split personality.

The three exchanged glances. "I don't think we're going to talk our way out of this one," Ryan whispered.

"Yeah, she seems a little crazier than the others we've come across," Beck suggested. "But we can handle them. We always do."

As the three henchmen went to confiscate their weapons and apprehend them, Vic head-butted the man in the nose, then drew his assault rifle. He shot the man in front of Beck, leaving Ryan to duck from shots being fired at him by another henchman. Vic quickly saved Ryan's ass with an incapacitating shot to that man's kneecap. He dropped to the ground in agonizing pain, and Ryan put a bullet in his head to end his suffering.

As bodies dropped like flies, Beck drew her Beretta and sent a few bullets toward the man atop the heavy-duty vehicle. One bullet hit him in the chest, sending him tumbling out of the seat in the turret. On his way down, he managed to squeeze the trigger of the machine gun, sending a few wild rounds down the highway, one of which landed in the back of his love, the leader of the pack.

With everything in disarray, the remaining henchmen's focus turned to their wounded leader.

Back at the truck, Alice whistled, sending Sgt. Peppers charging at the man holding her. He sunk his lengthy canines into the man's cheek. As the man released her and stumbled back, struggling to prevent the animal from ripping half his face off, Alice went for the truck and grabbed her machete.

Swinging, she went for the man that held her boyfriend captive, slicing his head clean off. Blood spurted all over Miles's body, soaking his face and glasses as the headless body plummeted to the ground. It was every bit the blood-bath Beck had predicted.

Next, Alice called off Sgt. Peppers. As soon as the German Shepherd released his death grip, Alice slid her twenty-four-inch blade right through the man's chest. Miles could see the edge of the blade slide out the man's back coated in a deep red liquid, drops of blood falling from the tip before Alice removed the weapon and let the body fall to the ground.

Miles was astonished. Who was this person? Was she the same person he had fallen in love with? Something from within made him feel like she had always been this person, just never had the opportunity to reveal her darker side. Maybe this is what real life had drawn out of her. Maybe it was time for him to rise up, too. He turned back toward the rest of the group, spotting Beck approaching the last one standing—the leader of the Crazies.

Vic and Ryan collected all of their weapons and ammunition that had been thrown about. The woman tried to crawl away, struggling to breathe with every inch she went. But Beck placed her foot atop the woman's back and applied pressure. She screamed in agony as her ribs pressed against the asphalt. Beck rolled over her slender body with the tip of her boot and looked her dead in the eye. Not a glint of shame or regret reflected from her soulless sockets. Kneeling, Beck ran her hand along the woman's cheek.

"I've seen this kind of shot before. Your lungs will slowly fill with blood. You'll suffocate before you bleed out." The woman started to choke as blood puddled in her throat. "Should I shoot you or let you suffer?" After a second, Beck walked away, not wasting a bullet on the wretched woman.

As Beck, Vic, and Ryan headed toward the truck, Miles tried to recollect himself. "Thanks for saving me," he said, removing his glasses to rid them of the putrid gore of the people Alice had just mutilated.

Alice cleaned off her machete on the henchman's clothes and placed it in the backseat of the truck to check on Sgt. Peppers. He barked at her as she approached him. Miles didn't think anything of it until he heard her yell out. Hearing screams of horror, Miles quickly returned his glasses to his face. Something had tackled her to the ground. The Silent Ones had managed to stray, leaving the pack from in front of the F-450 and slithering toward the sounds of the commotion the fight had produced. Alice was their first victim.

"Shit!" Beck said, drawing her handgun and putting the monsters in her sights. She blew the head off the first one, sending a splatter of disgusting, mucky blood onto the back of Alice's head, then aimed for the second.

Alice managed to roll over, but it was of no use. She was still held down by the sheer weight of the three atop her body. And to make matters worse, more were creeping closer by the second. Kicking and screaming some more, she couldn't break free. Miles reached for the henchman's gun on the ground and aimed at the monsters atop his girlfriend. He looked down the sight, put his finger on the trigger, and... did nothing.

What if I miss? What if I kill the only person I have left?

Those thoughts repeated over and over in his head. As he willed himself to just pull the trigger, Beck killed two more of the strays, and Ryan killed three. Finally, Miles backed away, dropping the gun as Vic emptied the rest of his assault rifle's clip into the horde, disintegrating them entirely.

"Oh my God! Oh my God!" Alice yelled, sitting up.

She rubbed herself down, searching her skin for any signs of a bite mark. The rest of the group rushed to her side with the weapons they'd collected in hand.

"Well, that was a close call, wasn't it?" Vic joked.

"This is no time for jokes, Vic," Beck said, holstering her Beretta.

Miles quickly dropped to his knees into the pile of mutilated intestines and rotting flesh next to Alice. He reached for her hand, but she shoved it away.

"I can't believe you didn't pull the trigger! What the hell's wrong with you?"

Miles understood why she was angry with him. Was she bitten? Did she know her time was coming to an end? He quickly tried to scan her body, but he couldn't see much of her skin under the copious amounts of blood that covered her.

Vic hoisted her up off the ground. "You're good, right?"

Alice, shaking, examined her blood-covered hands. "I think so."

"Good." Vic put the gathered weapons in the bed of the truck, then headed for the other vehicle.

"Alice, I'm sorry. I can explain."

"I don't wanna hear it," she snarled. Then to the others, she added: "Guys, let's just get back so I can clean up. The longer I'm in this filth, the more I feel like one of them."

Ryan followed Vic toward the heavy-duty vehicle the Crazies had—an RG-31 Nyala to add to their fleet. Beck, Miles, and Alice hopped into the F-450. Beck got in the driver seat, Miles sat opposite her in the passenger seat, while Alice, bundled up in a beach towel, stretched out in the back alongside Sgt. Peppers. Vic and Ryan followed behind them in the RG as they took off down the freeway, passing by the single row of dirt bikes, tire spikes, and the pile of fresh bodies.

13

Alice was the first to jump out of the truck when they arrived back at the compound. Miles could only imagine what was going on her mind. A warm shower and a fresh pair of clothes, most likely. But also betrayal. He knew she was upset with him. She had every right to be.

After getting the all-clear from Boyd, everyone headed inside. Miles followed Alice toward the bathroom, while Beck and the others reported to Serenity what they'd encountered before heading back out to hunt for game.

Though Alice and Miles left the group together, they parted ways once they passed the elevator. She went to rid herself of the ungodly stench of the undead, and he went upstairs to unload his belongings.

When Miles entered his sleeping quarters, there was no one in sight. Not one soul was even in the hallway. He threw his suitcase on the mattress and unzipped it. As he sifted through some old family photos he'd managed to slip into one of the side pockets, a slew of memories came flooding back; memories of his mother, who had died protecting him, and of his father, who had died because of his own terrible mistake. A cloud of bitterness lingered over his head.

Why am I like this? Why can't I just be normal? He dwelled in the pain as his eyes began to water. *I'm sorry, Mom and Dad. I wish things could've been different.* He took a deep breath. *I couldn't even save Alice. No wonder she's pissed at me. I gotta make it up to her somehow.*

He stood from the bed, slid the photos back into the suitcase, and kicked it underneath his bunk. Then he went to find Alice. Back on the main floor, he marched into the towel room and knocked on the bathroom door. He jiggled the knob, but it was locked.

"Alice, I hope you're not still mad at me," he said through the door.

Alice yanked the door open. "Never in my *life* have I been more upset with you, Miles. How could you just stand there and watch me get attacked like that? I needed you. I needed you to *help me.*"

There was so much steam in the room it resembled a sauna; it fogged the bathroom mirror and spilled out into the room in which Miles stood. Alice was wrapped in a towel, her auburn hair still damp.

The broken look on Alice's face told Miles exactly what he needed to do. He stepped into the bathroom and closed the door, then gently guided her to the edge of the tub, where he sat her down. He sat next to her and took a deep breath, collecting his thoughts. She seemed agitated and nervous, anxious even, but he assumed it was from her discontentment with his failure to be her white knight in shining armor.

"Look, Alice... I failed. I wasn't there for you when you needed me most. And I'm sorry for that."

Alice grabbed his hand. "Look, shit happens. I just wish you would've shot at least one of them."

"I would've, Alice. You know I wanted to, with all my soul. It's just..." He looked away for a second, gathering his courage to go on. "Alice, the reason I didn't shoot wasn't 'cause of my anxiety, or 'cause I don't love you enough. It was 'cause the last time I fired a gun, I shot my father."

"Was he already—?"

"No," Miles answered, anticipating that Alice was hoping Miles had shot his father as an act of mercy. "I killed him myself. It was an accident."

"Oh, Miles," Alice said, covering her gaping mouth with one hand.

There it was. He had finally admitted what he'd done to another human being. For the first time ever, he heard the words he so desperately didn't want to believe. He continued, "So I didn't shoot 'cause I was afraid I'd miss. I didn't shoot 'cause I was afraid for you. 'Cause I wouldn't know what to do if I lost you, too. The hope that you were out there somewhere, that I'd find you someday, was all that's kept me alive."

Miles reached his arm around her to express how much

regret and guilt he felt over the situation that had happened, and in return, she hugged him back, showing her gratitude. But as Miles caressed her moist skin, feeling her semi-damp hair brush up against his cheek, his hand brushed over something that felt unusual. He ran his palm back along her shoulder until he felt it again. Alice pulled herself from his embrace.

"What did I just feel?" he asked.

Alice recoiled and seemed to shrink before his very eyes. As she stayed quiet, refusing to answer, he spotted a speck of blood on the white bath towel she had used to dry herself off with. Then he gazed at his hand—at his fingers that were covered in something other than water. Tears welled up in her eyes.

Miles reached out to her to investigate the cause of the bleeding, but she backed away. Her quiet tears had turned into sobs. Turning away in shame, Alice grabbed her hair and moved it to one side, allowing Miles to see what she was hiding.

The bite mark above Alice's left shoulder blade was still fresh and red with blood.

Miles stared at her in stunned silence, but inside, he was screaming.

It's all my fault. Again! Now I'll be all alone. It's all my fault. Again! Now I'll be all alone.

Miles desperately wanted to speak, but nothing came out. In reality, there was nothing he could say or do that would change the situation. Alice had been bitten and that's that. He needed to at least tell Alice he was sorry, something he hadn't had a chance to do with either of his parents, but Alice spoke first.

"I guess this is goodbye, Miles."

He gasped. *Goodbye? Now? Why?* Then he remembered what Dr. Raines had said when he'd asked what would happen if someone got bit: "We'll take care of them." He'd feared the worst then. He was sure of it now.

Miles clenched his fists as he stormed out of the bathroom into the other room. Alice called out to him, but he ignored her. He punched at the cinderblock wall, then instantly regretted it as the pain shot up his arm. He shuddered at the thought of losing Alice—of her being killed all because she was infected. All because he had hesitated to pull the trigger.

She was all he had left. He took a deep breath to calm himself, but it didn't help. Maybe reaching out to someone he trusted for advice might be better.

———

IT WAS ALMOST noon when Miles finally reached the top flight of Smith Tower. Boyd stood outside on the observation deck, Remington in hand, scoping out whatever he could for target practice. Miles opened the sliding glass door, his nerves tightening up again.

"I heard y'all got into some trouble earlier," Boyd said.

Miles nudged his glasses up onto the bridge of his nose.

"Yeah, we did. That's actually what I wanted to talk to you about."

Boyd lowered his weapon and set it against the railing, then focused his attention on Miles.

"Today, I almost lost Alice." He shifted his weight onto the railing and looked out at the bay. "It's all my fault. If I didn't hesitate, then maybe... maybe things would be different."

"How so?"

"She's mad at me for not saving her when she got tackled by the Silent Ones. That's what I call them. The... you know. But I had a real reason as to why I didn't act."

"And you explained that to her?" Boyd looked out, spotting a large hawk fly by.

"Yes. And now she's no longer mad at me. But in the end, I still failed her just like I failed my parents. They're both dead now 'cause of me, and now I'm gonna lose her just the same."

"Lose her? How?"

"Ugh." Miles stumbled over his words. He had said the wrong thing, failing to keep quiet about Alice's misfortune. "Sorry, I meant to say now I'm afraid I'm gonna lose her."

Boyd rested his hand on Miles's shoulder and gave it a fatherly pat. "Look... in life we all lose people we love. It's inevitable. After seeing it on television and in movies, you'd think we'd get used to it, but for some reason, we don't. And that's why we need to cherish every waking moment we still have with those people, so when they do pass, we have something to remember them by; something that will help us push on."

Miles remained silent, taking in all of what Boyd had said. He knew Alice was infected, but he couldn't accept it. She was the only other person on earth he truly knew and could trust, and now she was leaving him. And to think, not even two days after finding each other once again.

3

ALIENATION

14

That night, in the dining hall, everyone was enjoying their dinner—everyone except for Alice. Miles could tell she was weak from how she was hunched over her plate and by the ghostly pale color of her skin. Even her eating was sluggish. During everyone's cordial exchanges, she kept quiet mostly—*mhmm'ing* and nodding during the conversation as if she didn't want to be there.

Miles tried to keep everyone's attention off Alice with simple small talk, hoping they wouldn't notice her health diminishing right before their eyes. It was working for the most part, but when her head started bobbing, he knew what was about to come next. His mother had gone through the same motions.

Alice silently stood from the table and staggered toward the hallway. She squeezed at her core, leaving Miles to watch in terror. While he hoped those around him would assume it was tonight's venison disagreeing with her, he knew it was the virus beginning to take effect. When nausea struck, she leaped like a lineman to a quarterback toward the nearest trashcan and vomited in front of everyone. It was both embarrassing and incriminating. All the witty banter and friendly chatter around Miles ceased.

"You okay?" Dr. Raines asked. She had come up behind Alice and placed one hand softly on her back.

"I'm fine," Alice slurred through the acidic salty taste in her mouth. "It's nothing."

She wiped a small chunk of God knows what from the corner of her lips, flicked it in the trash, and regained her balance. Dr. Raines escorted Alice out of the room to the infirmary to check over her vitals, and Serenity immediately left the table to follow after them. After they'd gone, the comical conversations and positive vibes resumed.

"You better go check on your girlfriend," Vic suggested a few moments later.

Miles tensed at the situation that was about to unfold. It was clear from Serenity's sense of urgency to follow Alice and the doc out of the room that she was eager to find out what had caused Alice to vomit, and he'd gathered that a few other survivors had drawn their own assumptions as well.

———

WHEN SERENITY ENTERED THE INFIRMARY, she'd locked the door behind her. Miles hadn't made it into the room in time. Pressing his ear to the wooden door, he crouched and listened.

"What's the verdict?" Serenity asked.

"Temp is 103," Dr. Raines said, pulling the tube thermometer from under Alice's tongue. Next, she grabbed the otoscope, wedged open Alice's eye, and flashed it across her irises. Alice's eyes followed the bright light as the doctor moved it from left to right.

"I feel much better now," Alice muttered.

"Honey, you're not fine," Serenity said, gently brushing her hand through Alice's hair. "Let's get you checked out. Go on and strip for me." She patted Alice's thigh.

Alice started sobbing, her shoulders tensing as she stood and began to undress.

"You know you can tell me the truth, right?" Serenity gave Alice a hard look that defied her gentle tone.

Alice *mhmm'd* as casually as she could manage as she unlaced her shoes.

"Good. So once you got back and washed up, did you discover any bite marks on your body?"

Alice didn't want to admit the truth, but there was no sense in lying. Serenity had taken her in and saved her from the terrors outside, and besides, she was about to find the marks on her shoulder herself. Alice had to be honest with her. "Yes, I did." She slid out of her cargo pants.

No, Alice! Why are you telling them? Miles clenched his fist.

"Where?" Serenity asked.

"Here," Alice said, turning around and pulling off her thermal, revealing the bite mark above her shoulder blade.

Not only had Serenity given Alice a glimmer of hope—especially when it came to reuniting her with her one true love, Miles—but she'd also given her a sense of purpose. Her work in the compound had given her a reason to continue to push forward in a world that still simmered with unrest.

"Open up!" Miles shouted, following a ferocious knock at the door. The knob jiggled repeatedly along with the banging. Miles's heart was racing faster than a speeding bullet. "Please!"

His voice trembled with fear and uncertainty as if he knew what ungodly things were happening within the infirmary. "Let me in, please!"

He could hear Alice's pleas for Serenity and the doctor to comply.

The second Dr. Raines unlocked the door to the infirmary, Miles rushed to Alice's side, hugging her with all his might. At the sight of Alice, in one piece and apparently unharmed, his heart folded over itself like an ocean wave from a boiling rage to a deep stillness.

"Is there anything you can do to save her?" he asked Serenity.

How could she allow Alice, her friend, a fellow survivor, a life saver to suffer the same demise hundreds of thousands of others had?

When he glanced at Serenity, her face, red with anger, said it all. Serenity wasn't happy with her findings—that

Alice had been infected and, maybe even more importantly, that she had kept it from her.

"Unfortunately, there's nothing we can do, Miles. I'm sorry." Then she looked directly at Alice. "Why didn't you tell me as soon you realized you were bit?"

Through tears, Alice answered. "I don't know. I guess I was in denial."

Miles squeezed Alice's hand tighter. "So now what?"

With a bottle of saline and an irrigation syringe, Dr. Raines tended to Alice's wounds to prevent further infection as the conversation continued.

Serenity clenched her fists, hesitating to answer. "Well, we're going to exile her from the compound to prevent the spread of the virus."

Miles's body went numb. "What?! You can't kick her out. Is this how you treat the people here?"

"Yes. She's receiving the same treatment as everyone else who's gotten bit."

Miles had thought the worst. Luckily, Alice wasn't going to get killed. Exiling her was better, but not by much. "There's gotta be another way. How about we quarantine her from the others? In a different wing or something?"

"We've tried that before, and it only led to more problems." Serenity pinched the bridge of her nose. "Miles, she's bit. She's *going* to die and turn—not tonight, but soon. She'll have to go. I'm sorry, but there's no other option."

"Can't you make an exception? For Christ's sake, she helped build this place!"

Serenity looked away in regret, heading toward the door.

Stopping in the doorway, she spun around. "There are certain rules to follow when it comes to surviving in this world. Making exceptions isn't one of them." She spun back around. "Alice, we'll pack up your things tonight, then send you on your way first thing in the morning."

With that, Serenity left the room. Miles had never felt such guilt before. Such anger. If it weren't for the trauma of his past, Alice wouldn't be in this predicament. It was all his fault.

Sitting there next to Alice on the treatment table, Miles tried to grasp what had just happened. Alice had been kicked out of the compound she'd helped create. He understood Serenity's logic; she looked at the bigger picture. The safety of the many was worth more than the safety of the few. More than a couple of measly teenagers. It made sense.

But it also sucked.

After experiencing his mother's slow demise, he assumed Alice had about the same amount of time. Seven days to live.

15

Miles didn't sleep a wink that night. Couldn't. He couldn't take his mind off Alice in fear a fellow survivor would dispose of her in the middle of the night.

It was 7 A.M. when he and a few others rolled out of bed. His eyes were itchy from the lack of sleep, his body in crumbling aches from the stiff mattress. There were only a few hours left before Alice would be forced out of the Underground. Forever.

Did it make sense to wait patiently by her side, to savor what little time they had left together? Or should he continue his quest for a way to keep her here—surely a fool's errand? Miles jumped out of bed and rushed out of the room in search of Serenity, not bothering to change out of his sleepwear. Assuming she'd be getting things ready for Alice to leave, he traveled downstairs to the infirmary where Alice had slept for the night. He was about to knock on the door when he almost crashed into Dr. Raines. She'd thrown the door open to leave and, by the look of her, it seemed she was heading somewhere important.

"Morning," she said.

"Morning. How's Alice doing?"

Dr. Raines took a sip from her mug. "She's stable. Still asleep at the moment, though."

Miles bowed his head, relieved that Alice hadn't been kicked out yet. "Umm, where can I find Serenity?"

"She's never in one place for too long. Doesn't even have an office. So, honestly, I have no clue." Dr. Raines spoke so quickly, Miles wondered whether she really needed whatever form of caffeine was likely inside that mug in her hand.

"Well, thanks anyway."

"No problem."

The two walked off in opposite directions.

There was no telling where Serenity could be. For all Miles knew, she could be up in the tower with Boyd. Hell, she could even be in the kitchen or the shower. He continued marching down the hall, his bare feet cold against the dark-colored marbled floors. In a stroke of luck, he soon ran into her getting off the elevator.

"Hey, I need to talk to you."

Serenity left the elevator and brushed past Miles, a box of supplies in her hands. "If it has anything to do with you wanting Alice to stay, my answer is still the same." She didn't spare a glance. "We just can't take the risk."

Miles followed after her. "Look, please, I'm begging you. She won't last a day out there by herself."

Serenity approached a utility closet, opened it, and

placed the box on a shelf. Miles followed her in. "She's a strong woman, Miles. She can handle herself."

He grabbed his head in agitation, then reached for Serenity's arm as she went to leave the room.

She quickly pulled from his grasp. "Look, I'm sorry about what happened to your girlfriend. Shit, between you and me, Alice has been a real help here. If there were any way I could keep her here, damn straight I would. But these are the rules. If you don't like it, then you can follow her right on out."

Serenity walked off, leaving Miles alone with his thoughts. Serenity's words echoed in his head. Not getting any sleep the night before had given him time to think of a possible plan—a plan so ridiculous that it might just work. There was one way to save the love of his life. Maybe. If what he had heard the man say about a possible antidote over the HF transmission two days prior were true, and if Miles could get Alice to the USCG base in Alameda, California in time to take it, maybe, just maybe, they'd have a chance to live their lives together the way they'd always planned.

Miles rushed upstairs to gather his things. He only had so much time before Alice would be discharged from the compound. More importantly, he only had so much time before Alice—

He shook the thought from his mind.

He had to be quick.

Miles slid his suitcase out from under his bunk and opened it. He threw everything he could live without on his bed and left everything he deemed useful in the bag. After looking at what he had decided to keep, he realized he didn't need much. All that was left inside were his two one-gallon jugs of water, a few clothes, some Polaroids, his bottle of anxiety medication, a few canned goods he didn't hand in to the chef, and a map of the Northwest.

There was no guarantee that the antidote would even be finished by the time he reached Alameda, let alone that it would save Alice's life. But it was worth a shot. And this was one shot Miles had to take. If he didn't try to save her this time, the weight of the guilt would end him. Miles pulled the map from his bag and walked across the room to a small wooden desk that stood in the corner. A quick search of the drawers turned up a red Sharpie, and though it had seen better days, there was enough juice left in it for his purposes.

Miles ran his pointer finger along what he thought was the safest route to Alameda: starting on Highway 5 for the majority of their travels all the way down to Sacramento, then onto Highway 80 to Oakland. From there, multiple routes could be safe, but they could just as easily be sketchy since he was unaware of the current status of the city.

He charted the rest of his route, and a backup one as well, before returning the map to his suitcase and leaving the room. In his mind, he had concocted the perfect plan.

Miles ventured down the hallway toward the elevator. He pressed the button and waited for the doors to open. When they did, he found Beck standing inside.

"Hey," she said, stepping aside to allow Miles to enter.

"I was wondering why the elevator went up instead of down."

The elevator closed and began its descent.

"I heard about Alice. How are you taking it?"

Miles leaned against the wall, trying his best to hold back tears. "Not so well. They're kicking her out."

"Yeah, I heard. It's going to be tough for her out there."

Turning to Beck as the elevator came to a halt on the first floor, Miles said, "No it's not, 'cause I'm going to be with her."

"What?! You're crazy." Then she took note of his suitcase and bag. "Well, I see you're not joking."

The elevator doors opened.

"I need to ask a favor," he said.

Beck walked out first, Miles following after her, the wheels on his suitcase squealing against the floor.

"Just hear me out."

His pits were starting to sweat. He wasn't going to allow his nerves to get the better of him again, even though he'd decided to save yet another pill for a more serious occasion. It was going on three days since his last pill. If he postponed his medication any longer, he ran the risk of losing his shit. He could crack in the blink of an eye. And he didn't want that to happen.

"I have a plan to save Alice."

Beck *mhmm'd*, venturing through the common area over to the armory to hand Sal a box of rubber gloves to use for cleaning all the weapons. "Oh really? I guess you're going to need a weapon then."

She nodded to Sal, hinting at him to retrieve Miles's baseball bat. Sal pulled it from the wall and handed it to Miles.

"Thank you, but that's not what I was talking about."

Miles's approach had been weak and frail. *If I'm going to get through to her, I have to be more direct.* Miles planted himself in front of the door, placing his arms against the frame and poking out his chest. "Look! I have seven days before the virus completely kills her—"

"And you know this how?" Beck interrupted, her arms crossed.

"'Cause that's how long it took for my mother to die. We've already lost one day. I can't waste anymore time. I gotta get to Alameda ASAP!"

"USCG's the only thing in Alameda, Miles. Why go there?"

"'Cause they've made an antidote. At least by the time we get there, they will have, I hope."

Sal couldn't help but comment on Miles's outlandish statement. "You know that's, like, 800 miles away, right? You'll never make it there on foot, kid."

"That's why I plan on taking the F-450 since you guys just acquired that other vehicle," Miles shot back.

"That's not going to happen," Beck said. "We lost our other two vehicles when some Crazies hit us a month ago. There's no way in hell Serenity will allow it."

Miles had to think quickly on his feet. If he didn't manage to obtain a vehicle, they'd never make it to California within six days. Then he remembered the dirt bikes they'd left in the middle of the highway. Miles leaned against the doorjamb and crossed his arms with confidence.

"How about this: Can you at least give us a lift to those dirt bikes we left on Highway 5?"

Everything was riding on that one answer. If Beck were to grant his request, then Miles would have a chance to save Alice. If her answer was no, he couldn't imagine what his next steps would be. Would he have to kill the people who reunited him and Alice? Would they kill him first? Would he be forced to put Alice out of her misery? He refused to think of such things.

Beck thought about it for a second, then answered. "You know what, that's true love. You're willing to risk your life for your girlfriend, knowing the chance you'll both make it is very, very low." She paused for dramatic effect. "Fine, I'll take you."

Miles lit up with gratitude. "Thank you. Thank you so much. You have no clue how much this means to me." He leaped toward Beck, wrapping his arms around her.

"Ohh trust me, I do."

Miles had everything he needed: his small backpack filled with some blankets and canned goods, his toothbrush, and a first-aid kit he had acquired on an excursion into town some time ago. His carry-on suitcase held the rest: the two gallons of water, his journal, and his medication. He was ready for a road trip with the woman he loved; it would have been romantic were it not for the circumstances.

When Miles went to check on Alice in the infirmary, he found Sgt. Peppers sitting by the treatment table in a guarding fashion, his ears pointy and alert. He eyed Miles as he slowly approached to wake her as if he didn't want anyone to disturb her. Miles wisely dropped to one knee and ran his hand over the dog's snout to keep relations friendly.

Hugging him, he whispered, "I'm gonna get Alice some help, okay buddy? I know you wanna come, but you can't. She's gonna be okay, I promise." Sgt. Peppers wriggled his nose under Miles's hand.

Miles wanted to believe so badly what he had promised the dog, but his mind lingered on the uncertainty of the situation at hand.

Alice sniffled, alarming both Miles and the dog. She slowly rolled over, revealing she had awakened.

"I hope you're not planning on doing something crazy, Miles."

Miles stood from the floor. "Alice, I can't let you go out there all alone. In your condition, that's a death sentence. You can't expect me to stand by and just watch you leave."

"You don't have a choice."

"I do. And I've made my choice. Now c'mon, we're going."

After transferring all of Alice's things into his suitcase and eating a breakfast he hoped would sustain him for the rest of the day, Miles loaded his bags into the Ford and helped Alice into the backseat. Sgt. Peppers followed them out to the truck, nudging and whimpering with every step they took, desperate to tag along. He bit and tugged at Miles's pant leg, urging them not to leave without him. He even barked a few times.

That's when Miles said to Beck, "Can you get him, please?"

"There's no harm in having him tag along," Beck said, lowering the tailgate so the dog could jump into the bed.

The time had come. The clock on the dash of the truck read 11:17. Miles buckled his seatbelt. He'd thought for sure it was earlier in the day, giving them more daylight to cross state lines with, but he'd been sadly mistaken. As they exited the parking garage and rolled down the road, all he could do was think.

I only have one chance to get this right—one chance to save her life.

16

Miles had dreamed of owning a bike before the *Great Reset*. He wanted to do the little things most motorcycle owners took for granted, like wash it and change the oil, and the big things, like long rides through mountainous back roads.

When he didn't receive a bike as his graduation gift, his hopes for doing such things started to dwindle. Then, when everything went to shit, owning a motorcycle was no longer a priority.

But the chance to ride was actually before him right now.

I'm only a few minutes away from riding, he kept thinking to himself as they drove down the highway.

When they arrived at mile marker thirty-nine, the truck came to a halt. The last time Miles rode was on Alice's father's motorcycle. He had allowed Miles to take his bike out for a spin two weeks after he got his license. God, was the feeling amazing, the wind blowing against his hairy arms and the sun beating down on his visor.

It didn't worry Miles that it'd been a while since that first solo ride. What did concern him was the outlandish idea he'd had that he could travel over 800 miles on a dirt bike with his sickly girlfriend as a passenger. And without the proper gear, no less. But they'd made it this far, and there was no turning back.

Determination was etched on Miles's forehead. He was prepared to do anything to save the person he loved most in the world—the only person he had left.

"Thank you, Beck," Miles said, peering out the passenger window. "Thank you for taking us. And thank you for reuniting me and Alice." He turned to her. "I don't know how much longer I would've survived out there with my shoulder messed up."

"Anything to help a fellow survivor," Beck said, staying vigilant to their surroundings to eliminate the chance of having another run-in with some Crazies or the undead.

"There they are." Miles pointed ahead out the window.

Both bikes were intact and in the same place they'd been left the previous day, right beside the pile of decomposing bodies. The place looked the same as they'd left it; the undead lying in the middle of the road and blood everywhere. Nothing had changed.

"You'd think someone would've stumbled upon those bikes, but I guess not many people are willing to travel the highway these days," Beck said.

Miles let out a slight chuckle. "Guess I'm lucky."

He opened the door and stepped out of the truck, grabbing his suitcase from the bed. He peered back at Alice in the backseat to check her status. Her skin was slightly pale and her eyes a bit swollen, but other than that she seemed okay. She had complained about immense pressure behind her eyes earlier—something of a scorching headache—but it was nothing a few ibuprofen couldn't help.

As Beck helped Alice out of the truck, Miles fastened his small suitcase to one side of the dirt bike and his backpack to the other using some bungee cords he found stashed in the door compartment. When he turned the key in the ignition to make sure the bike still powered on, he noticed that the fuel gauge near the speedometer read half full.

"There anything in the truck I can siphon fuel from the other bike with?" Miles asked Beck.

"Not that I know of." Beck lowered the tailgate and sat Alice on the ledge.

Miles considered their options. He had barely used one whole gallon of water over three days, but he knew Alice would need a lot more water than he did. They couldn't afford to waste the little they had. Still, the chances of coming across some gasoline for the bike along their journey were slim to none. And without fuel, they'd never make it to Alameda. Not making it to Alameda meant no chance of survival for Alice.

He unzipped his suitcase and pulled out a gallon of water. He took a long sip and handed the jug to Alice, who also drank her fill before he poured the rest out onto the asphalt. Then he went over to the other bike, shut off the peacock, pulled the fuel line from the bottom of the tank, and slid it into the jug. He turned the dial on the peacock again, allowing the light-greenish fuel to trickle out of the black rubber line and into the semi-translucent gallon until it reached the top. Miles returned and topped off his bike, then went back to the other one to refill the jug once more, getting every last drop of fuel.

Once everything was packed and ready to go, Miles helped Alice onto the bike, then took his place in front of her. He placed his foot on the kickstart pedal and gave it a push. The single-cylinder four-stroke motor came to life with a howling chug. He and Beck exchanged glances.

"Goodbye," he said.

Beck gave him a promising nod in return along with a gentle smile.

It's one down and five up. He remembered the mantra from his first time on a motorcycle. He was about to find out whether the gears were the same on a dirt bike.

"Hold on tight," he called over his shoulder. Alice closed her eyes, wrapped her arms around Miles as tight as she could, interlocking her fingers around his stomach, and rested her chin on his left shoulder.

Miles put the bike in first gear and eased off the clutch, the front wheel wobbling a little as he applied the throttle. He imagined Beck would be watching them ride off into the blistering cold, nothing but the puffy white smoke that spewed from the cold exhaust in their tracks.

The knobby tires on the dirt bike whistled against the wind, vibrating the frame of the motorcycle a little as they sped down the highway at fifty miles per hour. Miles assumed they could travel roughly ninety miles before running out of gas.

Taking into account the possible stops he'd have to make to use the restroom and to look for more fuel and food, it seemed to Miles that they'd never make it in time. But he didn't want to think about that. Miles didn't want to think about how life would be if he were to lose her, so he kept his eyes on the road, searching for any signs of danger as he swayed right and left, weaving in and out around abandoned vehicles and trash that flooded the road—things that were left behind by the many who'd succumbed to the virus.

———————

THE WIND BROUGHT tears to Miles's eyes. His glasses aided in keeping his visibility up, but it didn't compare to a proper, full-faced helmet. It was now 1 P.M. That left them about six hours to find a place to stay for the night before the sun set. If he were to get Alice to Alameda in time, he'd have to cover as much ground as possible before nightfall.

Another thirty minutes passed before they pulled into an old gas station. The place was eerie and desolate, yet somewhat unfazed by the surrounding environment. Its pumps were free of vehicles and its windows un-shattered. As Miles slowly pulled under the canopy near the front door, his eyes darted around to make sure the coast was clear. Once he felt they were in safe enough territory, he flipped the kill switch to the dirt bike and flicked open the kickstand with the heel of his boot. He held the bike steady to allow Alice to slide off safely first, then he dismounted.

He grabbed his bat from his backpack, then went for the door. There were no signs of any struggle; the glass in the doors appeared to be untouched. Miles tried to peer in through the cracks of the wooden-planked barricades on the inside of the door, searching for anything odd or out of place, but he couldn't see much. He cautiously pulled on the door frame, but it didn't budge.

Dammit. Locked.

"Stand back, Alice." He took his bat and bashed in the glass, then pried at a few of the loose wooden planks.

After a few tugs and kicks, they managed to break in, knocking down two planks with enough space for them to crawl through. Miles crept into the dimly lit room first, then helped Alice in when he was confident it was safe.

They both marveled at the fact that the place seemed undisturbed. Something didn't seem right. It'd been six months since the *Great Reset*, and this place hadn't been raided for its food. It was as if it'd been preserved in some form of historic capsule. Yeah, the outside looked worn down from the weathering elements, but the inside was pristine.

Alice clung to Miles's shoulder, looking around in the same fashion. "This is so strange."

"Strange indeed," he whispered back. "Imma see what food we can take. You need to use the restroom?"

"Not really, but I'll try."

Miles slowly led Alice down an aisle, their boots

squeaking against the worn checkered linoleum floor until they arrived at a door that had a female restroom sign planted on its face.

He was prepared to swing away if anything were to come charging at them as soon as he opened the door, but nothing did except for the horrid stench of long forgotten fecal matter that stormed their nostrils. The bathroom was void of light—blacker than a raven. He gave the solid oak door a quick knock with his bat, hoping there wouldn't be a response to the sound. And to his surprise there was nothing.

He flipped the light switch before entering, hoping the place still had power, but the old fluorescent tubes in the ceiling didn't flicker. *It was worth a try.*

As he stepped in, he could barely breathe through his nose the way the putrid smell lingered in the atmosphere. Miles inspected both stalls, making sure they were empty first before leaving Alice alone. He had trouble finding the first stall, hoping his face wouldn't collide with its sidewall. But after running his hands along the tiled walls he eventually found it.

He doubted she'd even want to use this bathroom, but he figured the men's was even worse. He propped open the door and left. As Alice got acquainted with the toilet, Miles searched around the store for anything he deemed useful. Sauntering down the aisles one by one, he picked out a plethora of dried snacks and bottles of water, placing them in the handheld shopping basket he had found in a stacked pile at the entrance.

They were lucky to find more canned vegetables and some expired granola bars, even a few cans of peanuts. But the real question was, how had this place remained untouched for so long? Miles couldn't figure it out.

Even though food and water were the main priorities, he had stumbled across a few extra items on his search around the store he felt could be useful: a flare gun he had spotted behind the clerk's desk, and a few off-brand T-shirts with moronic sayings that hung on a rack in the back near the ATM.

Winter was here, and neither of them had the proper gear to withstand the harsh temperatures. Alice was already suffering enough. If she were going to survive and beat the virus that was steadily taking over her body, Miles knew he had to keep her as comfortable as possible. He grabbed two shirts off the rack and slipped them over his head, then pulled the rest off to give to her before continuing his search.

After Miles finished aimlessly wandering the aisles, he heard a squeal in the corner of the station. *What was that?* In an attempt to stay calm, he inhaled deeply. Then he heard the sound again. He turned, finding the sound coming from the only place he hadn't checked—the back room.

He headed toward the door behind the counter. He didn't want to take the risk of getting attacked while his back was turned. So the only way to clear his suspicions was to open it.

He reached for the silver knob and turned it. A long screech followed the door as it opened, revealing a bleak office space. The stench was more severe than what he had smelled in the bathroom.

All Miles could make out in the shadows of the office was a floor safe, steel desk, computer, and a small desk chair. And above that, a venting window which had been shot in. Beside the desk were three monitors stacked upon one another that could've been the live feed for the security cameras.

A squirrel scurried up the wall and dashed out the window, drawing a gasp from Miles. He laughed and chuckled at himself when he realized the source of the ruckus, only to gasp in horror again when Alice came up behind him.

"Boo!" Alice giggled in satisfaction when she saw Miles jump out of his skin. When she saw that Miles was less amused by the trick, she changed the subject. "Look, I found a flashlight." She turned it on and shined it right in Miles's face.

"You're not funny," he said, but the smile creeping across his lips said otherwise.

"And you're no fun," Alice pretended to pout.

When she then turned the beam of the flashlight to scan around the room, the lightheartedness came to an abrupt end. Before them was a horrific scene.

Miles dropped the shopping basket.

"Oh my God," Alice said.

She quickly handed the flashlight to Miles, then turned away from the scene and covered her mouth and nose with both hands to prevent the onset of nausea from turning into vomit.

Miles stood frozen, the beam of the flashlight illuminating the body of a man who'd taken his own life with a shotgun to the head. His body had fallen against the wall opposite the computer desk, his blood and stringy brain matter clinging to the beige cinder blocks above his head. Witnessing the blank stare in the man's soulless sockets pulled at Miles's heartstrings. It was as if all hope had been lost—as if the man knew there wasn't an ounce of good left for him in the world. On his red vest, he wore a name tag that read manager. And in his lap, a leather wallet lay open to a pair of photos. Miles pointed the flashlight toward them to understand why the man took his own life.

As he inched closer, the pictures came into focus: the manager during happier times, enjoying the beach alongside people Miles guessed were his wife and newborn child. It was a sad sight to see, and Miles was struck by a feeling of kinship with the man, realizing he might have suffered the same demise if he'd been forced to survive much longer without reuniting with Alice.

"Miles, we need to go," Alice said, tugging at his forearm. "We've been here long enough."

But he didn't budge. The man's plight touched Miles deeply in a way that only one who has experienced depression could truly understand. He was thankful he'd chosen not to take his own life when he was at his lowest. Yet still, the thought of taking his own life lingered. Though it was the manager on the floor, Miles imagined he was looking at a version of himself, one who simply hadn't been as lucky. One from another dimension. From a place where he hadn't found Alice.

Alice pulled Miles away from the back room and lead him toward the front of the store. They were near the entrance before he managed to snap out of his emotional state. He turned and went back for the shopping basket he had dropped. "Look, you need to put these on." He motioned to the two shirts in his hand. "They'll keep you warm out there while we're riding."

Alice reached for the shirts. "You've always found a way to brighten my day, Miles. And for the longest time, I never understood why." She stepped closer to him. "I don't know if it's love, the apocalypse, or the fact that I don't have many days left that's making you do it, but I appreciate you risking your life just to try and save mine." Tears rolled down her cheeks.

"I'm not out here to try," Miles insisted. "I am here to save you, Alice. And I'm going to do it."

17

Time was of the essence, and Miles knew it. Alice was right; they had to get a move on. They could only dedicate so much of their time to snack breaks and bathroom stops. And the peanuts and granola bars could only fuel them so much; eventually, they'd need some real food, with whole proteins and healthy carbs.

Miles shook his head, brushing off his worries. He escorted Alice out of the gas station and back onto the dirt bike, loading all their tasty findings into their luggage before continuing down Highway 5. The lack of power to the gas station had made access to the fuel pumps impossible, but even if he could somehow manage to get the pumps working, he imagined they'd be as dry as the Mojave Desert. It was a blessing they'd been able to scavenge some snacks; he was ready to take the win.

Yet thoughts of where to find food and shelter lingered as they rode. Miles considered fishing, but without a pole, that seemed a weak option. Hunting with a baseball bat didn't seem too promising either. Trapping meant staying in one place and waiting for an animal to arrive, costing them time they didn't have.

Developing and rejecting these scenarios clouded his mind from the real mission in front of him. Before long, Miles had already reached the bottom of the gallon jug that carried the siphoned fuel from the tank of the other dirt bike left behind by the Crazies. Their options were limited: either stop and waste more daylight looking for fuel, or keep going and run the risk of being left stranded and vulnerable to the unforgiving world. They were in the middle of Castle Rock, and though Miles had read about the wonderful scenic views of Mt. Saint Helens, he had no time to appreciate them. Though few of the vehicles that lined the streets looked even the least bit promising, he pulled over anyway. He rolled onto the sidewalk next to a storefront and parked.

Miles helped Alice off the bike before opening his bag to fish out his map. "Stay here, okay? I'll be right back."

Alice nodded.

With the map in hand, Miles walked over to the entrance of the store and slowly opened the door. It was a post office. Small and quaint. Cautiously entering, he looked around, making sure the coast was clear. Feeling confident, he stepped in, approached the counter, and laid out the map.

Shit. He spotted two bodies on the floor behind the counter. *It's all good. Just stay calm.* As Miles checked over his plotted routes for reassurance of their intended direction, he hoped Alice had stayed put and didn't wander off to explore what the little town had to offer.

But when he peered out the window, he didn't see her. Alice was gone. Vanished. He panicked. Quickly folding up the map, he rushed out of the post office. He scanned his surroundings, looking for any sign of her whereabouts, but found nothing.

Shit. Where'd she go? He began hyperventilating. *God dammit! Why didn't she just stay put?* He'd go and look for her but didn't want to leave the bike in fear that someone would steal it out from under their noses. He also didn't want to call out her name to attract any unwanted attention since they were in unfamiliar territory.

Miles bit the bullet and left the dirt bike unattended in his search for Alice, but not before grabbing his bat. The small town looked like something out of a horror movie, something similar to the little town of Derry in Stephen King's *It*, which only made his fear of losing Alice even worse. Most of the buildings that ran along the street were one story tall with an exception of a few that had two. Some had horribly chipped painted brick and others had painted clay that had cracked away. And the crumbling asphalt beneath his feet showed signs of a lost battle against mother nature as patches of grass grew up from between the cracks. The little town had been left in complete disarray, with loose newspapers flowing in the wind, some left glued to the pavement.

As he walked along the premises searching for Alice, he found a few car doors left wide open. *Could this be Alice's doing?* He wasn't sure, but he took it as a sign and kept pushing onward, his trusty bat in hand ready to swing at anything that moved. He inspected those vehicles, peering into each to see if he could find anything worth scavenging. In one of the cars, he even found one of the Silent Ones inside, strapped in its seatbelt, its eyes ripped from its sockets. The monster was still animated, its body squirming, hands reaching for him as he tapped on the window.

Miles was about to turn left at the end of the street when a loud crash startled him. Miles's body jolted in fear as his head shot to the right. One of the small air-conditioning units that sat in the window of a nearby building had taken a fatal plunge. He exhaled deeply after spotting what had fallen. Then he looked back at the bike, checking to see if Alice had returned to it, but she hadn't. So he continued wandering further and further away in search of her. And sure enough, after he turned the corner onto another street, he found her. Alice was standing by a yellow school bus that'd been left blocking the main road, its emergency exit door left ajar.

He scurried toward her. "Why'd you leave? I told you to stay put."

"I figured I'd find us a place to sleep for the night."

Miles pinched the bridge of his nose and exhaled. "I planned on stopping in Portland, Oregon. That's where we'll sleep tonight."

"I'm tired of riding, Miles. Can't we just stay here?"

Every minute spent debating on whether to spend the night there in a bus or to continue onward led Miles to believe his efforts to save her were pointless. He needed Alice to trust him. "I need you to trust me on this, okay."

She sighed. "Please can we just stay here? I don't feel so well."

There was no use arguing. Alice didn't want to travel any further, and Miles no longer wanted to waste his energy pushing back.

"Okay. I guess we can spend the night here. But at sunrise, we're gone."

Alice beamed with contentment as Miles put out his hands, interlocked his fingers, and hoisted her up into the bus. He quickly ran back to the dirt bike and rode it over to the vehicle so he could lock their belongings away with them for the night.

Though they could've easily used one of the many buildings as shelter instead of a school bus, in hindsight the confined space made it easy to keep tabs on both entrances so there'd be no surprises in the middle of the night. It was now 3 P.M. and with about two and half hours left of daylight, Miles decided to hunt for fuel as Alice turned the bus into a makeshift hotel for the evening.

He returned to the bike and rode around a few vehicles until he stumbled across a police cruiser. *That looks promising.*

Before starting their trip to Alameda, Miles had salvaged the fuel line from the other dirt bike to use as a siphon. He pulled the bike up next to the spout of the vehicle and flicked out the kickstand before dismounting.

Miles cautiously approached the vehicle. If luck were on

his side, the door would be unlocked. If it wasn't, and the car's battery still had any juice, he'd run the risk of setting off the car alarm. He closed his eyes and pulled the handle, hoping for the best. To his surprise, the door opened. He exhaled in relief. He pulled the lever near the seat, and the gas cover sprung open. Miles unscrewed the cap, slipped the hose in, and drew a few breaths to get the fuel pumping.

Miles's heart soared when the first drops trickled out of the hose, but it sank just as quickly when no more drops followed. The hose, he realized, was only a foot long, drastically shorter than the inlet pipe that ran down to the actual tank of the full-sized sedan.

Shit. This isn't gonna work. I need a longer hose.

As if in answer to his prayers, he looked up and discovered a True Value hardware store right across the street from where he stood. He knew the place had exactly what he was looking for, he just needed to muster up enough courage to step inside and find it.

Reaching for his backpack to grab his bat, Miles headed toward the building. When he peered in through the window of the entrance, he spotted no movement. He took a deep breath and pried open the powerless sliding glass doors with his bare hands, creating enough space for his body to squeeze through.

One, two, three, breathe. One, two, three, breathe. One, two, three... He stepped inside. The storefront faced the sun, which shined inward illuminating a good portion of the interior. As Miles tiptoed past the cash registers, taking short strides toward Aisle 6: PLUMBING, he noticed a few Silent

Ones in Aisles 3 and 4. His grip tightened around the handle of the bat as he tried to slither by unnoticed.

He continued past Aisle 5 and rounded the corner of the plumbing aisle only to realize he was no longer alone. Miles stopped in his tracks, the rubber on the soles of his boots squealing against the worn linoleum. The bastard was in the middle of the aisle right next to the translucent ten-foot-long hoses that he needed to get his hands on.

The monster growled, turned toward the sound of the squeaky shoes, and stared straight at Miles. The former store employee had cloudy eyes that were lifeless and dull but dusted with an ounce of demonic nature. His skin was grey and soggy as if it'd been deprived of circulation for months, and his clothes bore rigid holes, exposing the infected gunshot wounds he had taken some time ago. The man dragged his feet as he trudged toward Miles.

With his fingers sweaty and heart fluttering, Miles didn't loosen his grip on the bat. He raised it over his shoulder and prepared to send the monster's head out of the park. He patiently waited as the man approached, limping at a decent pace, then he pulled back. *Just a few more seconds.*

Swing!

The nails on the end of the bat made contact with the man's jawline, sending his body crashing into the cream-colored metal shelving, then onto the floor, followed by an avalanche of goods collapsing over him. Babe Ruth would've been proud.

Miles knew it'd only be a matter of seconds before he'd

be enclosed on both ends of the aisle by the others, despite their snail-like pace. So he made a mad dash for the hose, snatching it from the shelf, then sprinting down the aisle, almost knocking over one of the undead on his way out of the store. He squeezed through the entrance, barely giving himself a minute to reclose the sliding glass doors behind him.

The rush of adrenaline that had fueled him recklessly encouraged him to reopen the doors and knock off a few others, but his rational mind worked to control the urge. If he took such an unnecessary risk and got bit—contracting the virus—he, too, would no longer be in any shape to carry on. The prospect of yet another failure was all he needed to snap himself out of the barbaric state he was in.

Miles quickly returned to the police cruiser, slid the hose down the inlet pipe and into the tank, and retrieved enough fuel to refill both the bike and his gallon jug. His mission had been a success.

One day. One day back together, and now she's gonna die. Why? What have I done to deserve this? Why couldn't I have been the one to get bitten? Now I'm gonna lose everything. By tomorrow morning, we will have lost two days. By my calculations, that gives her five days left to live. And that's only if her body reacts to the virus in the same way my mothers did.

I hate how Alice fought me on spending the night in Castle Rock. Why can't she just trust me and follow my lead? She might be delusional. My mother fought with me about going out to find food when we ran out. Though I didn't wanna leave her, either, I knew we needed something to eat. Maybe Alice just doesn't want me to get tired. I don't know.

Being tired is the least of my worries, though. Being hungry is what bothers me most. All we had today was a can of green beans and some crackers. It wasn't much, but it made do. I hope when we get to California, they'll have some actual food for us to eat. That's if we even make it there. No. We are going to make it there. I've got enough fuel to get us another hundred miles or so, but that's still 600 miles shy of Alameda. I just hope I can get her there in time.

Sincerely, M.W.

P.S. I think my biggest fear is even if we do manage to make it there in time, they won't have an antidote.

18

After dinner, Miles cuddled next to Alice in a sleeping bag and began to reminisce about all the times she was there for him and how she had helped him get through so much. His first memory was from one year earlier.

Classes had just ended that day, and the bus ride home was embarrassing. It had been another day of defeat. Miles walked the driveway and went inside. Ignoring his mother's 'good afternoon' greeting, he stormed down the hall into his room and closed his door. He barely heard the doorbell ring before he threw himself down on his bed and finally allowed the tears to fall that he'd been holding back all day.

Suddenly his door flew open.

"Go away, Mom," he said, his face buried in his pillows. "I don't wanna talk right now."

And after he said those words, he expected to be left alone—his bedroom door to be re-closed. But that didn't happen. Instead, a sudden sound of feet against carpet rushed his ears, followed by a heavy weight crushing his bones.

"Ouch," Miles said, rolling the person off him.

As soon as he saw the auburn hair draped beside him, he knew his assailant was Alice. She rolled back over to give him a kiss, but he turned away. Then she noticed his soaked cheeks.

"What's wrong, Miles?" she asked, running her hand along his back in a motherly fashion.

He didn't respond.

"C'mon, spill it, what happened?" She wrapped her arm around his body and pressed her face to his.

He turned and sat up, revealing a black eye.

She gasped. "Not another fight."

Miles *mhmm'd*. Readjusting himself—turning over to rest his back against his headboard—he sighed. "It's like no matter what I do, I still get beat up."

Still lying on her stomach, Alice lifted her head and cradled it in her palms. "It's okay, Miles. The fact that you tried to fight back is all that matters."

"But that's the thing, Alice. I didn't try to fight back. I just ran like a coward. If it wasn't for Coach Windsor breaking it up, both of my eyes would probably be black."

"Well, have you tried looking up some videos on how to fight on YouTube? My dad looks up videos all the time when he wants to learn new things. It might work for you, too."

"You know what, you're right! I never thought of doing that." Miles fished out his cellphone from his pocket and searched 'how to defend yourself' on YouTube. The plat-form yielded a plethora of results.

Eddie and Rick won't know what's coming to them.

Alice situated herself beside Miles against the headboard, joining him as he picked out a video. An hour later, they were both practicing hooks and sweeps in the backyard. Even though neither of them had a clue as to what they were doing, Miles still enjoyed her company and uplifting words.

Another memory of pleasant times with Alice popped into his head. It was when they went to the movies for their third date. Alice parallel parked near the theater and watched for traffic before opening her door.

"I'll get the tickets," Miles said, opening the passenger door. "You get the popcorn, okay? Then meet me at the usher."

A car passed by, and she opened the door. "Got it."

And as soon as they entered the building, they found it packed. They exchanged glances, then got to work. Miles got in line behind some heavyset man to grab their tickets as Alice got in one of the many lines for popcorn. When Miles finally purchased the tickets, his bladder shot a message to his brain.

He glanced over at the concessions stand, spotting Alice still two people behind from ordering. They locked eyes. He beamed with a chuckle as she rolled her eyes. Then he motioned to the bathroom. And after he relieved himself, he returned to the main lobby of the theater to find Alice yelling at a man he'd never seen before.

He rushed over. "What's going on?"

"He knocked the popcorn out of my hand!" Alice exclaimed.

Miles glanced at the bag on the floor and exhaled. The kernels were everywhere, the fake butter soaking into the carpet.

"If you weren't in the way, that shit wouldn't have happened, bitch!" the guy said.

All hell broke loose.

"What'd you call me?" Her tone was stern.

Alice took her soda, removed the lid, and tossed the drink over the guy's head, dousing him in the dark brown liquid. The entire lobby went silent.

"What the fuck?!" the man yelled.

"Don't you *ever* call me a bitch!" Alice shouted, pressing her finger to the man's chest. "Matter of fact, don't you *ever* call *any* woman a bitch!"

Miles chuckled silently, trying not to wake Alice beside him. *God, did she do a number on that guy. I remember it so vividly. Could barely get her off him.* He glanced over at her and brushed her hair out of her face. Tears began to form. *There's so much I didn't get a chance to say, so much we didn't get to do together. Why do things have to be this way?*

The streets were quiet; the sky was dark with grim. The sun hadn't quite peeked over the mountain yet but was due to show soon. Miles awoke first, moving carefully about the bus so as not to wake Alice. He glanced nervously out the window up at the surrounding sky after a strike of thunder roared nearby.

The clouds had shed unforgiving tears throughout the night, but the streets had dried considerably by the time he had awakened. Only patches of damp pavement masked the streets now. But the cloud cover and the thunder told Miles a torrential downpour was on the way, and he knew it'd be damn near impossible to ride any further in it without the proper gear.

Miles reached in his backpack, pulled out his medication and a gallon of water, and threw one back. Peering inside the medicine bottle, he updated his mental countdown. *Two more left.*

Afterward, he glanced over his left shoulder to admire Alice in what he thought would be a blissful state. Instead, he could see there was a serious change in her health. Her eyes flickered underneath her lids from left to right as if she were having a nightmare, which caused her breathing to be unsteady and quick-paced. Her body squirmed continuously, never relaxing. He rested his hand upon her forehead and found that her skin was boiling—sweating even.

I'm running out of time.

Miles didn't want to wake her, but he knew it was for the better. He leaned in and kissed her on the forehead, then whispered in her ear. "Hey, wake up sleepyhead." Alice slowly came to as Miles brushed his hand through her hair. "I hate to break it to you, but there's no time for breakfast. There's a storm front headed this way. If we leave now, we'll beat it."

Alice struggled to lift her whole body from the hard floor they had slept on. Her movements were weak and sluggish. Miles could see her shiver. The temperature outside was thirty-three degrees, making the steel bus even colder inside. Miles knew Alice wouldn't want to leave the cozy warmth of his cotton blanket, but if they were to get to Alameda in time, they'd have to stay on schedule.

With no breakfast to fuel her body, Alice dragged her feet as the two gathered their belongings. Miles grabbed the blanket she'd used the night before and turned around to tuck it back in the suitcase. But when he turned back toward her, he found Alice convulsing in the middle of the aisle, her mouth foaming and head banging repeatedly against the floor.

"Alice!" he shouted, rushing to her aid. Dropping to his knees, he quickly rolled her onto her side so she wouldn't choke on her vomit and cushioned his hand under her head to prevent any further possible trauma.

Don't do this to me now! C'mon, you're tough. Fight it! He watched in terror, waiting for the seizing to end. After a minute more, her motions finally came to a halting stop. But she didn't wake. "Alice. Alice?"

He tapped her cheeks, but her body was non-responsive; completely numb. He ran his finger under her nose to see if she was still breathing. His shoulders relaxed and his heart rate slowed when he felt the gentle release of air brushing against the fine hairs on his finger. He wedged open one of her eyes and examined how milky-yellowish they looked. She wasn't dead, but she was in some sort of comatose state that was going to make travel impossible.

And now with it being the start of the third day, her time was getting closer. There was no way they'd be able to continue on this journey in the way they had. Now with her unconscious and incapacitated, Miles had another hump to overcome. He gathered the rest of their belongings and packed them up. He then dove deep in thought.

I could drive the bus, but that's only if it has enough fuel and a good battery. But this thing is huge. We'd stick out like sore thumbs. I don't wanna attract that kind of attention. I could leave her and come back with the antidote. I could cover more ground that way. No! That's stupid. If anything were to happen to her while I'm gone, I wouldn't be able to forgive myself. God dammit!

Miles had no choice but to leave Alice behind in search of a better vehicle. *I'm gonna miss that bike. But it was great while it lasted.*

He grabbed his bat and began surveying the area, inspecting all the vehicles left behind. Some had flat tires, others had been totaled in accidents. Some were in perfect condition, but their owners had taken their keys with them when they fled, making them no good to Miles. He didn't have the slightest idea how to hotwire a car, and he was sure Alice didn't either.

Miles had walked nearly a mile when he spotted a mechanic shop in the distance. He instantly remembered the wall full of key hooks at the shop where his father used to take the Ford Ranger for tune-ups and inspections. He hurried toward the building, his heart racing, wondering what he might find inside—what unimaginable things he might come across.

When he reached the entrance to the shop, he peeked through the glass door and spotted a figure milling about in the lobby: a female dressed in navy coveralls. Miles knocked on the glass to draw the monster toward him, glaring at the half-jawed woman in disgust. Her left arm was missing, and her mouth was black from the periodontitis that had rotted away half her teeth. He took a deep breath and opened the door, holding it open to allow the bloodthirsty woman to walk through. As she came stumbling out, he backed away slowly, raising his bat behind his head so he could hit another home run.

Decapitation wasn't the goal, but it happened as a result of the extent of the mechanic's decay. Her headless body dropped like a sack of potatoes, but her head remained hooked on the sharp nails that protruded from the bat's end cap. Miles gave the bat a quick whip, and her head flew off into the shop's parking lot.

Miles entered the mechanic shop, the door closing behind him with a heavy thud. He scanned his surroundings for any other monsters that might appear from the shadows and quickly realized the shop was too large to search on his own; time wasn't on his side. So he did what he had to do—something he thought he'd never have the balls to do—he began to make as much noise as possible in an attempt to draw any remaining Silent Ones toward him for immediate dispatch. Miles banged his bat against the register and knocked over the magazine display that lined the wall, calling out to any unseen predators to make their move.

Only seconds passed before Miles saw not one, but two of the undead wander out of the back room toward the commotion. It didn't take him long to take them out, but by the time he was done, his shoulder had begun to ache.

Miles scurried across the scuffed linoleum floors and behind the counter, where he grabbed every key off the rack. Then he headed for the garage. Three cars were inside: one up in the air on a lift, the others on the ground. Only one of them looked worthy of the 600-mile drive. He inspected the tire pressure and oil level on the Honda Civic before praying to God the battery had enough juice left to turn the car over. He sat in the driver's seat, put the only key bearing a Honda insignia in the ignition, and turned. The car turned over slowly, but fast enough to ignite the fuel in the cylinders.

Miles had done it. Another successful mission. All he had to do now was grab Alice and hit the road.

He quickly hopped out of the Honda and used the thick ropes to hoist up the garage door. By this time, dark clouds covered most of the sky, not allowing any sunlight to escape. He couldn't even tell what time of day it was. All he knew was that he and Alice had overstayed their welcome in Castle Rock.

———

MILES HAD DRIVEN BACK to the school bus and picked up Alice, strapping her in the backseat before removing his suitcase and book bag from the bike to put in the car. After that, the drive was long. With no one to talk to, Miles grew bored. *Guess this is what being a chauffeur feels like*, he tried to joke. Then he caught a shiver. The Civic's heat was busted. Radio was, too, not that any stations would be broadcasting over it anyway. Their newfound vehicle was a piece of junk. The only thing good about it was the safety it brought —in the form of shelter from the rain beginning to fall. They were now rolling at sixty miles per hour down Highway 5 on their way out of Castle Rock. The next stop was Portland.

The rain wasn't letting up. The roads were surprisingly clear of debris for the most part. There weren't many abandoned cars blocking their path. It was pretty much a straight shot all the way, especially now with Alice unconscious. Miles didn't have to worry about stopping anymore for her to relieve herself frequently, one of the many symptoms that followed infection with the virus.

In better times, Miles would like to have thought they were positioned to make great progress. But he knew things weren't like they used to be, that anything could happen. A flat tire, a deadly encounter, a horde of the undead. The best thing he could do now was keep a low profile and stay positive.

The pair had been on the road for forty-five minutes when Miles thought he spotted something in the distance. As the car got closer, he could plainly see something—someone—standing in the middle of the freeway. Miles applied the brakes, bringing the car to a dead stop.

It can't be.

———

A QUARTER MILE down the road stood a pickup truck. A 1991 electric orange Chevy Blazer with a six-inch lift kit: large, knobby radial tires with white lettering: and a license plate that read KING ED.

The driver's-side door swung open, and Eddie stepped out. He walked to the hood of the Chevy and perched on its bumper, his M-16 assault rifle in one hand and a beer in the other. "Looks like we've got a live one," he said.

The passenger door to the Chevy opened, and Rick stepped out. "Great!" he said, wiping the drops of rain from his forehead. "Been awhile."

Eddie aimed his rifle toward the car and looked down the magnified sight, then scoffed. "You won't believe this."

Rick came up behind Eddie. "What? Some old lady or something?"

"Even better." He handed Rick the gun. "Take a look-see."

Rick eyed down the scope. "I thought for sure he'd be dead."

Eddie downed the rest of his beer and belched, crumpling the can and tossing it in the ditch. "Shit, you and me both. Gotta give him props for making it this far."

"Hell yeah. Too bad he won't make it any further." Rick pulled the trigger, launching a bullet toward the Honda.

———

POP!

A bullet shot out the front tire of the Honda Civic.

"Fuck!" Miles's eyes widened as fear set in. He swallowed the lump in his throat. *This can't be happening.* In all that's happened, he thought he'd never see them again. He reached for his bat in the passenger seat and exhaled all his fears. *There's no point in running anymore.*

Miles kicked open the door and stepped out, leaving an

unconscious Alice in the backseat. *They probably think I'm alone. I can only hope.* His heart was racing now. He was unsure if the tightness he felt in his chest was from being scared or from a panic attack. Nonetheless, at that moment, he cared more about Alice's safety than his own.

The rain started picking up even more now, his hair and clothes getting drenched. He looked down to keep the rain out of his eyes and continued praying, hoping they wouldn't put a bullet in his head. When he looked back up, he found the truck creeping toward them.

Miles thought of Alice in the backseat. *I'm gonna get you outta here if it's the last thing I do.* As the truck got steadily closer, he knew he couldn't run now. It was impossible for him to escape. He was on a single-lane road with nothing but wasting farmland and eerie forest around him.

Eddie and Rick had had it out for Miles since the first day of high school. He'd endured countless beatings at their hands, some of them brutal. And now that there were no longer any laws, nothing was stopping them from killing him. If he wanted to keep Alice safe, he knew that this time he would have to fight for his life—and hers.

Miles stepped away from the Civic and stood his ground, keeping his eyes wide open as he heard the motor of the truck rev up. He assumed they were going to do a hit and run, attempting to make his body tremble with fear before running him over. But at that moment he no longer felt scared, but rather calm, ready to accept his fate. Miles never thought that this would be how he'd go. If anything, he assumed he'd die the same way as Alice, by the virus that had taken the lives of so many.

But as he continued walking toward the approaching truck—waiting for the sudden impact from being run over—he didn't feel the raging heat from the v-eight motor nor the excruciating crunch of his ribcage making contact upon the front bumper of the Chevy. He kept walking, but the impending doom he so desperately tried to prepare for didn't happen. Eventually, the truck slowed to a stop, leaving six feet between them. He stared both Rick and Eddie down through the front windshield, trying his best to ignore the rain pelting his face. Miles had won the game of Chicken.

Eddie kicked open the door and got out. "Well, well, well... look who we have here."

Miles rolled his eyes. "Do you really wanna do this?"

Eddie drew a pistol and pointed the barrel at the crease between Miles's eyes. "I never thought I'd see you again. And now look, here you are."

"This is the part where I ask you what you want." Miles's tone was thick and strong.

Eddie chuckled. "You already know the answer, Miles. There's no reason to ask anymore. You should see the look on your face. Still looks the same as the last time we saw each other."

Miles stepped closer to Eddie. "Must be the light." He brushed the barrel of the pistol out of his face. "What are you guys even doing out here anyway? It's kind of far from home, don't you think?"

"We're out here living the dream," Rick announced, stepping out of the truck. "There's nothing else to do but explore nowadays."

"Then why bother me? Didn't you get enough fun back in high school?"

"Oh, Miles. You don't get it. You never did—"

"No, you never did!" Miles shot back. "Both of you!" This was his first time standing up to Eddie and Rick. Granted, it was under extreme circumstances, but regardless he was now doing what he had wanted to do for the longest time; be a man. Stand up for himself.

Eddie repointed the gun at Miles. With it to his head, his life flashed before his eyes. Miles could see himself now: punching Eddie right in the jaw and knocking him out, taking his gun and shooting Rick, leaving him to bleed out, then stealing their ride to continue on their journey to Alameda. But that didn't happen.

Miles did punch Eddie in the jaw though, with his left hand, but it fell flat. As a result, he dropped his bat to tend to his aching hand.

Eddie rubbed at his chin. "Oh, you've done did it now." He regained his balance, then kicked Miles in the balls.

Miles dropped to his knees in agony, falling to the wayside.

Eddie looked him dead in the eyes. "Karma's a bitch, ain't it?" Then he crashed the butt of his pistol against Miles's skull, completely knocking him out.

"Good one," Rick said, walking over to the Honda to see what else Miles had acquired, only to find a girl in the backseat. "Hey Ed, check this out." Eddie left an unconscious Miles on the ground as he went to see what Rick had called him over for. "Isn't that, that one chick from school? What is he doing with her?"

"Beats me. But I know what *we're* about to do with her."

20

"This is gonna be great," Eddie said, standing at his truck's tailgate while untangling some rope. Rick was silent as he stood beside Eddie, untangling another. They both were standing in the long drive of a two-story suburban home the size of a mansion. The place was a sight to see, with two pillars lining the porch, large bay windows, a three-car garage, and stonework highlights. It'd surely be a magnificent dream home if people were still alive and living in dream homes.

"You really think we should be doing this?"

Eddie shot Rick a *what the fuck* look. "Of course! Why not? It's been a month since we've gotten any." He turned and headed toward the front door of the house. "We wouldn't be doing this if Rachel didn't split."

Rick closed the tailgate of the truck and followed Eddie into the Portland residence. "Yeah, I know, but don't you think this is going too far?"

Eddie turned to Rick and scoffed. "Hell no! I deserve to have some fun. And you do, too. Now c'mon, stop wasting time."

Eddie marched passed the dining area and headed down the basement staircase. With every step they took, a creak followed until they landed on the cold concrete. The unfinished basement was dark with little light peeking through the two hopper windows. Eddie took his lighter and walked around the open area, lighting every candle he came across. One by one, the area grew brighter, revealing Alice and Miles both tied up and still unconscious. The orange hue from the flames brought warmth to Alice's bare skin. In nothing but her bra and panties, they had tied her up at all four limbs between the studs of a frame suited for double doors.

Alice's body hung limp-like; her skin cold to the touch and the wound on her back growing more and more infected by the second.

"You sure you wanna do this? Remember, she's been bit." Rick motioned to the bite mark above her shoulder blade.

"So. Until she turns, she's just like everyone else." Eddie approached Alice and smacked her across the face to wake her. She didn't come to. He tried again, this time her body jolting in response. She finally awoke.

The look on Alice's face when she awoke showed she had no clue where she was. She looked around, staring both Eddie and Rick down. But it didn't seem like she could see them. She took a deep breath, then a second later her eyes adjusted to the dimness. Eddie and Rick stood in her presence. She tried to move, but couldn't. Then she inspected her hands and feet to find she had been tied up. Then she shivered, noticing she was in nothing but her underwear. She got scared. Miles was nowhere to be found. It was just her and two guys from high school.

Her knees trembled in fear. "What the hell is this?"

Eddie smiled. "Why hello there. I'm glad you're awake."

Who would've thought Eddie and Rick would stoop to such a level? Tying up an innocent girl; planning to do God knows what to her.

"Where's Miles? And where are my clothes?" she demanded.

"Don't worry, he's right behind you, watching," Rick answered. "But he's a little tied up at the moment."

"And as for your clothes, well they're hanging right over there," Eddie added, pointing his pistol toward the clothes-line across the room. "But you won't be needing them anymore. See, ever since the world went to shit, we've been kinda craving something more, if you catch my drift." He reached for Alice's jaw and massaged her cheekbone with his thumb. "Yeah, the killing and stealing's fun and all, but there are just certain needs that need to be met."

It couldn't be, could it? Are they talking about—

Alice shuddered.

She yanked her head from his grasp. "Fuck you!"

"That's not nice now." Eddie nodded to Rick. Rick turned and grabbed a roll of duct tape from the wooden workbench and tore off a piece. "We're only trying to make this experience as pleasant as possible for you, that's all."

"*Please*. Nothing about this is pleasant." Alice tried her best to dodge Rick from covering her mouth with the duct tape, but to no avail, failed as her limbs were already preoccupied.

She struggled to break free, mumbling screams through the tape, but it was of no use. As Eddie took his finger and ran it along her neck down to her navel, she pulled and jerked her body away from his menacing touch. She tried to kick at him, but the ropes only had so much slack.

By this time Miles started to come to, finding himself tied wrists to ankles in a corner of the room near the air-conditioning unit. "What the fuck?!" he shouted. When he looked up to find his girlfriend getting taken advantage of, he struggled fiercely against his bindings.

Eddie turned to Miles as Alice froze in shock to have been found in such a vulnerable state. "Nice of you to join us. You're just in time for the show. Would you care to do the honors?" He pointed at Alice's panties. "Oh wait, you can't." He laughed.

"Miles!" Alice mumbled through the tape, her words barely audible. She started to cry.

"Did they do anything to you?" Miles asked, knowing whatever her answer would be, he still wouldn't be able to understand it.

She continued trying her best to communicate through the tape, but still nothing.

"So help me God, if you guys don't let her go now, I'll—"

"You'll what?" Eddie interrupted. "Look at you, tryna be all protective. If I ain't know no better, I'd say you *finally* grew a pair of balls." He turned to Rick. "Isn't that something?"

"It sure is," Rick shot back.

Eddie whisked his hands through Alice's dark auburn hair to calm her. "Shhhh. No need to cry. It'll all be over before you know it." He wiped away her tears with rough, blistered hands. "Besides, you might like it. Bet you ain't never had a *real* man before." He shot a glance over her shoulder straight at Miles.

"You bastards! You're not gonna get away with this," Miles yelled, squirming around on the floor.

Eddie positioned himself behind Alice and ran his finger along her waistline. She cried, squirmed, and shook, trying to dodge his callused hands, but failed. After a few more seconds of taunting, he ripped her panties off, then smacked her across the face to shut her up. But it only made her whimper and sob more. He tucked his gun in his back pocket, unzipped his denim jeans, and slid them down to his ankles.

———

AS EDDIE TRIED to get a hard-on, Miles watched in terror and utter silence, knowing there was nothing he could do. All hope was lost. But then, out the corner of his eye, he spotted a handsaw nearby among a few other scattered tools. It must have been left behind by whoever framed the basement. With Eddie and Rick occupied, he inched toward the saw.

Alice already didn't have much fight in her because of the virus raging through her bloodstream. Fighting back would only exhaust her energy stores. She tried to prepare her mind for what was about to happen.

Eddie was ready. He put his left hand on Alice's head, grabbed a handful of hair, and tugged as hard as he could, causing her to arch her back and yelp in pain. Miles only had seconds to act before Eddie would violate his girlfriend.

Eddie was inches away from penetrating Alice's womanhood when a blunt object crashed against the back of his skull.

Miles's eyes darted toward the sound.

Eddie fell to the concrete floor, grabbing at the back of his head in pain. When he looked up to see what had hit him, he found Rick standing over him, his pistol in his right hand.

"What the hell, Rick?!" he yelled.

Rick touched his gun to his scalp in confusion. "This isn't right, Ed." He started pacing. "It's one thing to do it to someone who's down for shit like this, but rape... this is just fucked up, man."

Eddie checked his fingers for blood, making sure his scalp wasn't bleeding. "Is this about going first, 'cause you can go if you—"

"Shut up!" Rick shouted. "Just look at her." He ripped the duct tape from her mouth and pointed her face in his direction. "She's already bit and looks as sick as a dog, and now you wanna torture her some more." He shook his head in shame. "You're sick, man."

Rick turned around to think of what to do next. "I get you wanna make Miles suffer, but there's gotta be a better—"

That was as far as Rick got his sentence before a blunt object cracked his skull wide open, sending his body crashing onto the workbench, knocking over two candles onto a pile of mothballs in the corner of the room.

"Oh, shit!" Eddie exclaimed, struggling to pull his jeans up.

Miles had managed to escape in the nick of time. A fire burned from within him as he glared at Eddie, his hand tight on the hammer he used to kill Rick with.

Eddie was stunned. Shocked even. In disbelief. It took him a second to realize what had happened. But by the time he did, Miles had already struck him in the head—twice. He continued bashing Eddie's skull into a pulp.

When Miles was finished, he stood over the bodies of Rick and Eddie, a hammer clenched tightly in his fist. He'd been disgusted at first by the blood spraying from Eddie's caved-in skull, but now the sight felt right. Good, even. They were dead now. They couldn't hurt him anymore. He looked from one to the other, trying to scrum up some remorse. He hadn't wanted it to come to this, but he had to adapt if he and Alice were going to survive in this new world. It was one thing to kill the undead, but to kill people who were alive and well was a different story. Nevertheless, he was now free of the burden he carried. The pain and stress that lingered over his head for years. For if he hadn't taken the initiative, things might have ended differently. They might have died after enduring Eddie's torture; whether from a gunshot or by being fed to the Silent Ones. Only God knew.

Miles had to snap himself out of his brooding, as he was already facing a new, deadly problem. He and Alice were in a basement surrounded by flames that were steadily rising.

"Help! Miles!" Alice exclaimed.

She had spotted the flame making its way toward the two-by-four stud she was strapped to. The fire was rushing toward her, and she was still tied at all limbs. Her efforts to break free were useless. She didn't want to die naked and helpless.

"Miles, you gotta do something, *fast!*"

The fire trailed the bottom frame of the wall toward her, and the heat was starting to radiate off her ankles, sweat bubbling from her pores.

Though Miles's hands were shaking from the two murders he had just committed, he managed to regain his composure enough to start untying the ropes that held her feet.

"Hold on! I'm gonna get you outta here." Smoke started to accumulate, rising to the ceiling and up the stairs to the main floor.

One, two, three, breathe. One, two, three, breathe. One, two, three... Miles watched the ever-growing flames illuminate the room around them as he continued working on the stubborn knots. In his efforts to free Alice, he didn't pay attention enough to the flames burning close to his feet. The cuffs of his jeans caught fire. *Shit!* He quickly patted his pants leg to put out the flame, but not before burning the cuffs of his jeans, leaving them black and frayed.

"*Miles!*" Alice managed to get out after a cough.

By this time the fire had risen an inch away from her right wrist. Miles heard the quivering tone in her voice. He had untied the ropes at her feet, giving her an edge when it came to pulling free, but not enough. With his pants no longer on fire, Miles finished the job, untying the last two ropes holding her hands.

As soon as Alice was free, she dashed for her cargo pants and boots. Unfortunately, her shirt had already burned to a crisp. Now wasn't the time to get dressed, however; they had to find a way out of the engulfed basement first. Much of the framed structure around them was already gone, doused in an orange hue. They could barely see. The smoke had turned to fog. Embers and ash floated around them, nicking their skin with every touch. Death lingered in the air. The supports in the ceiling started to char and creak from the heat. It was time to leave, but there was no exit.

The staircase was in a blaze, and the two hopper windows were too high to reach. Alice squeezed the life out of Miles's hand, but adrenaline numbed him against the pain. Through coughs, he tried to calm her. "Don't worry. We're gonna make it outta here."

He scanned his surroundings—the smoke burning the whites of his eyes—hoping to find a stool or chair, but instead found a heavy wool blanket folded up on the floor next to the water heater. *Thank God.* In a panic, they rushed to the blanket, wrapped themselves up like a burrito, and dashed up the stairs and out the front door. Safe at last.

The view of the burning suburban home was nothing remarkable, but rather a reminder of what could've been. Still wrapped in the blanket, Miles and Alice watched from the tailgate of the Chevy as the house burned from the inside out. Maybe it was a good thing it caught fire: it'd be the perfect burial ground for Rick and Eddie. The perfect place to delete the people of his past he tried so hard to forget. But one thing that wouldn't disappear in the ruins was the nightmarish memory they shared of Alice almost getting raped.

A strong gust of wind chilled them both to the bone, sending them to furl even deeper into the wool blanket. With nothing but the clothes on their backs, they were doomed, set to fail. They had lost everything: their clothes, food, water, medical supplies, weapons, and most importantly, the map. The only thing that could get them to Alameda.

A feeling of major setback sank in as the house fire continued to rage uncontrollably. If it were any consolation, they did have the Chevy Blazer at their disposal, though Miles extremely despised it simply because of the wretched memories it brought. Nevertheless, they had something.

Miles exhaled a sigh of pain. "I give up."

"What do you mean?" Alice questioned, noticing the dreary tone of his voice.

"We've lost everything, Alice. If I would've just pulled the trigger when I needed to, we wouldn't even be in this—"

Alice shushed him with her finger. "That's all in the past now, Miles. Don't beat yourself up about it. We're here now and we've got each other. That's all that matters."

She trapped his hand in a loving snare to calm him as best she could. But he snatched his hand away and stood from the tailgate.

"But now we're stuck," he said. "I have no clue where we are or if we're even safe right now." He turned away from her. "I feel like everything I've done to try to save you has only set us back."

"But at least you're trying, Miles. At least you're trying."

21

Katherine Belford was ready for Oregon's harsh winter. She was making her way back home from gathering the last of the firewood she had chopped when she spotted an enormous smoke signal off in the distance. It was mid-afternoon—three o'clock to be exact—when she saw it. As she peered over the clouded tree line, wondering what had caused the fire, she noticed the gentle flakes of snow beginning to fall. Winter had finally arrived.

She continued pushing her wheelbarrow across the field, the collar of her winter coat and long grey afro-hair whisking in the cold breeze. Her joints ached from the cold, but it wasn't anything some whiskey couldn't fix.

From her years in the air force, Katherine had learned that liquor was the best jacket. She had put in enough work for the day; now it was her right to kick back with a bottle of Jack Daniels and one of the old romantic comedies she had seen a dozen or so times before on her portable DVD player. It was the only thing to do to pass the time since the world went to shit.

Katherine hung her axe on her home's exterior and placed the freshly chopped timber in the log rack on the front porch before stepping inside. She unlatched the rein-forced door to her two-story farmhouse when an explosion shook the ground on which she stood.

Boom!

Katherine spun around to find a huge display of debris falling from the sky above where she had seen the smoke. "What the hell? That's gon' draw lots of attention."

She marched inside and grabbed her .308 Winchester rifle to scout the location of the explosion. She couldn't see a thing through the scope. But she knew it in her bones: some-body was out there. She scurried over to her 1968 International Harvester and parked it in the barn behind her home, hiding it from whoever might be looking to scavenge a vehicle. Katherine did not visit her old friend Jack that night, nor did she turn on her old DVD player. Instead, she patiently waited in her late husband's leather recliner, gun in hand, to see if any visitors were going to pay her a visit.

———

LARGE FLURRIES of snow crashed against the windshield of the Chevy Blazer. Miles drove cautiously through the sprawling neighborhood, desperately looking for any sign that could help lead them in the right direction. The glass was foggy, the dash heat on full blast. Alice shivered under the blanket. Even now, wearing a shirt Miles had given her, she pressed her hands to the vents for warmth.

They were only a few blocks away from the house when the explosion happened.

"Thank God we left when we did," Miles said.

"We'd be charred like smoked brisket," Alice noted with a giggle.

As they continued down the road, they spotted more of the Silent Ones peeking out from the shadows.

"You seeing this?" Miles muttered.

Alice *mhmm'd*.

The undead were crawling out of every nook and cranny imaginable and were stumbling toward the location of the explosion.

Alice gasped as one of them clipped the Chevy and fell to the ground. "Be careful!" she blurted out. "We don't want to be stuck out here with these things."

Miles glanced over at her peering out the window. "Alice... do you wanna talk?"

She turned to him. "Talk about what?"

"You know, what happened back there." He placed his hand on her thigh.

"I'd rather not."

"I couldn't possibly know what it felt like, but..." he paused, unsure of what to say. "Just know that I'm here for you if ever wanna talk about it."

She took his hand in hers, and as she did, it grew warm.

Miles's heart, too, warmed at the thought that he and Alice were in this together and that nothing and no one could tear them apart.

As they continued down the road in search of shelter and a safe place to gather their thoughts, Alice peered out the window, watching as they passed one hobbling figure after another. They eventually came to a four-way intersection where the truck eased to a stop.

After a few seconds of silence filled by the gurgling exhaust of the truck, Alice said, "That way," pointing to the left.

Miles wondered how Alice could be so sure until he followed her gaze. An old man stood next to a stop sign pointing them in that direction. The man was bug-eyed, disheveled, with tattered clothes. His entire body was covered in blood. But what was even more strange was the woman he had tethered to him. She looked like many of the others who'd died and come back: her body decomposing, showing bone, one arm missing. But why wasn't she attacking the man? Ripping his face off? Eating his lower intestines for lunch? These were questions the two pondered for many minutes after.

Before long, Alice snuggled up in the blanket and closed her eyes to catch up on some long-overdue sleep. She tried to drift off to the slow swaying motions of the Chevy as it weaved in and out of the sea of the undead. She was just about to fall asleep when Miles slammed on the brakes, jolting her forward until her seatbelt yanked her back.

"What's happening?!" Alice said.

Miles was too stunned to answer. When Alice followed his gaze out the front window to see what had stolen his breath, she, too, fell silent with a gasp.

The wreckage of a 747 Boeing jet lay in their path, having taken out a majority of the surrounding brush about a mile south only to finish its impact in the middle of the neighborhood. Its wing had been ripped off, exposing its interior and spewing its contents about the area—suitcases and purses hanging in the trees. The gaping hole revealed many bodies still strapped in their seats—some straining futilely against their seatbelts.

"And I thought I'd seen it all." Miles shuddered at the ungodly sight.

"Look at those people," Alice said. "All those lives, gone." She grabbed his hand. "To think, those people probably never imagined dying that way." She turned to Miles. "I'm so afraid. I don't wanna die, Miles." Then with a pull, she encapsulated his entire body in a loving embrace.

Their hug was ended abruptly when a bloodied hand plastered a print across the driver-side window, scaring them both. Miles pressed the accelerator pedal to the floor as a reflex and took off toward the plane. But there was no clear passage for them to travel. At the last second, he yanked the steering wheel left, sending them directly into the woods toward a tree. In a panic, Alice jerked the wheel in the opposite direction to prevent a head-on collision.

Crash!

They'd just missed the large evergreen by a few feet, but

in turn, jumped a fallen log and landed in a deep creek behind the plane, Chevy's chassis left to teeter on a boulder, its rear end suspended above the water and its front buried in the rocky channel. One axle was broken, as was the truck's horn, which blared ceaselessly into the night: a dinner bell for the undead. They were sitting ducks.

Miles had cracked his face against the steering wheel, leaving him with a bloody nose and a minor concussion. If he didn't know any better, he'd think it was game over, but something inside him made him wipe the gushing liquid from his nostrils and kick open the door. He unfastened his seatbelt, then went for Alice's.

"C'mon, we gotta go," he said warily, hauling her out from the driver-side.

Alice was awake but disoriented. "Where? Where are we going?" she managed to get out, stumbling over the creek's rocks as he pulled her through the water.

He could barely hear her over the blaring horn. Once they'd made it through the shallow creek, he hoisted her over his shoulder and started up the hill on the other side, getting as far away from the plane and the wailing truck as they could.

DAMMIT.

Miles didn't want to admit it, but he was lost. They'd trekked about two miles in the woods and found no signs of life. No homes, vehicles, or stores. Nothing. He could no longer hear the Chevy, nor the monsters that had surrounded it. While he was happy to have put some distance between him and Alice and those dangers, now he feared that in his efforts to do so, he might've created a new set of issues.

The snow was coming down heavier now, beginning to stick to the ground, covering the fallen leaves and debris from the previous autumn. The clouds hovering above even darkened the sky a little, giving the trees the illusion of ghoulish creatures from hell.

Maneuvering through the maze of the forest, Miles continued to search for any signs of life—*real life*, not whatever the hell had taken over the majority of the U.S. population. Fears raced through his mind: frostbite, bear attack, starvation, dehydration. He didn't know which was worse, but he knew that if they didn't find shelter soon, they'd both succumb to one of mother nature's many dangerous attributes. He prayed for a miracle and pleaded for mercy, hoping it would improve their chances of survival. But mother nature hasn't always been forgiving.

Step by step they hiked, continuing up another hill until they stumbled upon a narrow trail. They followed it to an opening in the trees, which revealed a wide-open field with a large farmhouse on the far end. From a distance, Miles could see no light protruding from the windows. Yet the area around the house seemed well-kept; it didn't look decrepit the way most places do in this changed world.

With Alice more alert now, she was able to carry her own. They both crossed the field, hoping what they'd find on the inside of that house was nothing more than peace and tranquility; a place where they could recoup from the events of a long and terrifying day.

22

The weathered wood creaked as Miles stepped onto the front porch. His eyes darted between the front door and the front window, wondering what, if anything, could be waiting for them inside their potential shelter. The hairs along his arms lifted as the crippling thought of them being watched popped into his head.

Alice clung to his side and slowed her breathing as best she could. Miles put his ear to the door in an attempt to hear anything rummaging around inside. The entire house was quiet; he could hear nothing but the constant thump of his heart within his chest. Next, he peered in through the window of the old wooden door to see what was inside. Still nothing. He stepped away from the door, bringing his focus to the nearest window. Unfortunately, he couldn't see much through the thick curtains. He walked closer, cupping his hand around his eye to keep his reflection from blocking the view, and squinted to get a look through the narrow gap between the two curtain panels.

There she was. A Black elderly woman, sitting in a chair, aiming a gun right at him.

"Duck!" he yelled.

He dropped to his knees, dragging Alice down with him. They scrambled off the porch and onto the grass and hurried toward the back of the house, hoping to find a place to hide.

"What did you see?" Alice asked.

"An old woman with a gun," he whispered.

Suddenly, the sound of a cocking weapon made Miles turn to stone.

"State your biz," Katherine said firmly, her rifle aimed at the back of Miles's head.

Alice spun around her palms to the sky. "We're just lost and looking for a place to spend the night, that's all. We don't want any trouble."

"And why should I believe you?" she said.

Miles slowly turned and held his hands up. "'Cause, we're just teenagers in need of some help. But if you don't wanna help, that's fine. We'll keep moving. But if there's anything you can spare, please—"

"These are tryin' times, boy," Katherine said. "And I ain't into donating."

The three stood like statues in the blistering cold for longer than anyone would've preferred. Katherine saw the teenagers' bodies begin to shiver from lack of proper clothing, and she noticed that the frightened looks on both faces never waned. She lowered her weapon, surprising no one more than herself.

"Well," Katherine began. "If y'all were wanting to kill me, you'd have done it by now. Might as well get you inside." She quickly motioned them back toward the front of the house and opened the door, allowing them into her humble abode.

"We are sorry to bother you," Miles said. "When we didn't see any lights on, we didn't think anyone still lived here. We won't stay long."

"No, bother... it's fine." Katherine closed the door behind them and turned the bolt lock. "I haven't had any visitors in a long time. I sure could use the company." She beamed. "You're welcome to get comfortable on the sofa in the living room if you'd like. I'll be right back." Katherine headed upstairs.

How could an old woman like her survive this long, out here, alone? Maybe she has skills we don't know about. But something doesn't seem right. Maybe she's not alone. Maybe someone's expected back at any minute. Whatever's going on here, I don't plan on sticking around long enough to find out.

Miles went for the door and toggled the bolt lock. The staircase steps creaked and cracked as Katherine headed back down. In a panic, he pulled open the door, grabbed Alice's hand, and ran out.

"Wait, what's the hurry?" Katherine asked, spotting them darting out the door.

Miles didn't look back as they made their escape off the front porch. But Alice slipped from his grasp. He quickly turned to find Alice walking back inside, where the woman stood at the bottom of the stairs holding a navy blue cashmere sweater. She handed it to Alice.

Miles stood there in the snowy grass as the woman looked at him with patience. "The weather's only gon' get worse, hon. You'll freeze to death out there. And if the wolves don't get you, whatever those things are out there most certainly will."

There was no way Miles could take back what he had done. He'd made himself look like a complete fool. An asshole really, but in this day and age, it was to be expected. You can't trust anyone you meet. He remained silent as he marched back up the steps and into the house with his head held low. The woman turned the bolt lock behind him once more, then went for the living room.

"Now that we've established that I ain't gon' do y'all any harm, how's 'bout I introduce myself? I'm Katherine. What're y'all's names?" Katherine plopped down in her husband's leather recliner.

"I'm Alice and this is Miles."

Katherine noticed Miles standing with his arms crossed as if he was uncomfortable being in her home. "I ain't gon' bite, honey." She gestured to him to take a seat. "Go ahead, join your friend." Miles gave in and took a seat. "Well Alice, it's a pleasure. A pleasure to meet you both. Since the storm's just begun, it looks like y'all gon' be spending the night."

The sky had already dimmed, leaving a majority of the house dark. The large bay window overlooking the snowy field was the only thing keeping the place somewhat lit. As Alice slid the sweater over her head, Katherine stood from her chair and went for the fireplace.

"Y'all look starved. I was just 'bout to cook dinner. Y'all ever had venison?"

She dropped in three logs, sprinkled some lighter fluid over them, reached for the box of matches on the stone mantle, and brought life to a flame. Heat soon followed.

Though Miles didn't hunt alongside his father in all his years, he sure partook in enjoying whatever Rodger had managed to kill and cook up for dinner during the season. Alice too enjoyed the delicacy.

Miles scratched at the back of his neck. "We love the stuff. Is there anything I can help with?" He stood from the couch. "It's the least I can do for you letting us spend the night."

"As a matter of fact, you can fetch a few more logs from the front porch," Katherine said, heading down the basement steps.

Miles walked out the front door and grabbed another three logs to place next to the ever-growing fire, then returned to the couch. When Katherine returned from the basement, she had a large, wrapped slab of chilled meat in her hands. She entered the kitchen, grabbed a large cutting board, a knife, and some skewers then returned to the living area.

"I know this ain't the normal dinner y'all are used to, but in these tryin' times, it could be worse." Katherine handed each of them a skewer, then split the slab three ways.

"There's seasonings in the cupboard if y'all want some. I put mines on after it's cooked." She grinned. "Gives it more flavor."

The grated rack above the fire glowed red. Katherine placed her skewer on the rack first—the meat hissing as it made contact—then Alice and Miles followed her lead.

"Y'all want rice, or will some greens do?" Katherine disappeared back into the galley-style kitchen to grab a mason jar of collards from one of the cabinets.

"No thank you, the greens are fine," Alice said, snuggling under the thick blanket that was draped over the back of the couch.

"So... Katherine, is it just you here?" Miles asked, taking note of the multiple family photos hanging on the wallpapered walls going up the staircase and above the mantle.

"Unfortunately. I've been alone for the better part of a decade now. My son was the first to go." Alice gasped, expecting the worst of reasons. "That smart little bugger. I was expecting him to grow up to be just like his daddy, living off the land and being a provider to the townsfolk. But he had other plans."

Katherine poured the contents of the mason jar into a small, lidded, stainless-steel pot, then returned to the living room to place it over the fire. "He went off to school and got a degree in law." She sat back down. "Last time we spoke was the day of the outbreak. Said he was gon' come back home." She glanced out the bay window and sniffled. "I guess he ain't make it."

"I'm so sorry."

Katherine turned to Alice. "No need, hon. No one's meant to be in our lives forever."

Those words struck a chord within Miles. *No one's meant to be in our lives forever.* He didn't want to believe it, but that statement rang true. Looking back at all that had happened the past six months, everyone he adored so much was dead: his parents, his favorite teacher, his friends—hell, even his girlfriend would be dead soon if he failed to get her to Alameda in time. Katherine was a wise woman. He was hesitant to ask about her husband, in fear that she'd drop more bombs of uncomfortable wisdom on him. But he did anyway.

"And your husband?"

"Died of a stroke one day out in the field, 'bout nine years ago. It was the alcohol that did it. He loved to drink. Some days I feel like I'm to blame for that." She shot a regretful glance at the bottle of Jack Daniels sitting on the end table beside her. "But that's all in the past now."

She flipped everyone's skewers over, then stirred the boiling pot of greens. "Enough 'bout me, though." She crossed her legs and fell deeper into the leather of the recliner. "Spill it! I know y'all are running from something."

Miles and Alice exchanged a quick glance. They needed a cover story fast.

If Katherine found out why they were out in the middle of nowhere so far from home, she might not be so kind as to let them stay the night. Maybe they both wouldn't wake up the next morning. Maybe she'd grab her Winchester and shoot them both dead right there in the middle of the living room.

"We figured no better time than now to travel and go sightseeing," he blurted out. "We had made plans right before the outbreak, no need to cancel them now that the world is in shambles. We're on track to California." Miles had told the truth, just not all of it.

Katherine only needed to know where they were headed, not that they were on a tight schedule. If any hint of Alice being a carrier of the virus was to surface, there was no telling what would happen to them.

———

BY SIX O'CLOCK, the sun had set, and the night was growing colder. Two inches of snow had stuck to the ground already, and more was coming.

"Thank you for the food," Miles said, heading off to the kitchen to wash their plates in the sink.

"Yes, thank you," Alice added, warming her hands with a hot cup of tea.

Miles had never had authentic Southern food before. The way those greens tasted was something he hoped he'd never forget.

"It's nothing. Like I said, I don't get much company and haven't for a while. You know, since the world went mad." Katherine grabbed her bottle of Jack Daniels and poured herself a glass. "Speaking of goin' mad, I gotta say y'all have some balls, traveling out here alone."

"Well, we were more prepared before we met you," Alice said. "We just ran into some trouble. Ended up losing everything: our clothes, food, water, medical supplies, and even our vehicle."

Katherine's brow raised in wonder. "Hopefully that explosion earlier had nothing to do with it."

Miles dropped his glass into the sink in shock. The last thing he wanted was for Alice to relive what had happened in that house.

"Well, actually, um..." Alice stammered.

"Not really, but we were in the area when it happened." Miles took over for Alice as he came in from the kitchen. "Yeah umm... that was right around where we lost our stuff. Ran into some old friends that weren't *really* our friends, if you know what I'm saying."

"I understand. People can be so cruel sometimes."

Alice scoffed. "Yeah, tell me about it."

JOURNAL ENTRY #46:
TUESDAY, DECEMBER 12TH, 2023

Well, I've lost pretty much all hope now. It's been three days since it happened. I don't know where to turn exactly. Alice almost got raped. We both were almost killed. Hell, we crashed the truck and were almost lunch meat for the Silent Ones. I'm blessed to still be alive, but at what cost? I'm thankful that an old lady was kind enough to let us stay the night here in her old farmhouse, but I'm unsure of her agenda.

I'm afraid that if we tell her the truth, she might kick us out. Or even worse, kill us. I don't know really, and I don't wanna find out. I just want to get to Alameda. But now the weather has picked up, and the snow is coming down hard. I don't think we'll even make it in time. Especially now that we don't have a vehicle.

God, why does everything have to be so difficult?

And with everything that's happened, I lost my medication, too. I wish I could just take the rest of the pills and drift off into oblivion. Maybe I should just give up. Take the old lady's gun and put Alice out of her misery. Then turn it on myself. What am I talking about? I can't kill myself now. If I do, then this whole thing would've been all for nothing.

But now I don't even have my medication. Can I even make it to Alameda without it? God, I sure hope so.
Sincerely, M.W.

iles awoke to a troubling sound. It was still pitch black outside when he overheard Alice struggling to breathe. From what he could make out, it sounded like she was coughing up copious amounts of mucus into the toilet down the hall from the room they slept in. She was getting worse, and there was nothing he could do about it.

I hope she doesn't wake Katherine.

He heard her again. Could it have been the venison? Or the virus? Whatever it was, if she were to keep expelling fluids like this, she'd no longer have enough energy to continue their journey.

Relighting the candle on the nightstand with a lighter Katherine had left for him, Miles rolled out of bed. He crept down the hall toward the bathroom. With the candle in his right hand, he gave the bathroom door a gentle push with his left. He stepped in and found her hunched over the commode, her body shaking from chills and her hair covering her face like the girl from *The Grudge.*

He shined the light over the commode, then over her body, only to find that what he'd assumed would be mucus coming out of her mouth was actually blood. He quickly rested the candle on the vanity and dropped to one knee as he reached for Alice's shoulder.

"Are you okay?" he asked.

Her body was cold to the touch. He slowly brushed the hair from her face so he could wipe her mouth clean with a towel. But when he did, he found her face covered in maggots. In shock, he fell back, crashing to the floor. He couldn't believe his eyes.

Suddenly, a dark liquid drooled out of her mouth, and she started to crawl toward him on all fours. He frantically tried to stand and escape, but she grabbed ahold of his ankle and pulled him back to the floor. By the time he was able to turn around and look her dead in the eyes, she was inches away, ready to take a bite out of his cheek.

Crunch!

The bite jolted Miles out of his sleep. His clothes were drenched in perspiration, and his heart was racing. He grabbed at his chest. It felt like he was having a heart attack. Maybe the little bit of alcohol he'd had with dinner was responsible for bringing on the wretched nightmare, or just the amount of stress he'd been under lately. Regardless, he glanced to his right and found Alice still in a deep slumber on the couch, as calm as could be. He exhaled in relief, thankful that what he'd witnessed was not reality.

He looked at the fireplace and saw nothing but a few embers floating up from the ashes. He had no clue what time it was but knew the fire needed to be brought back to life. He lifted himself from the hardwood floor, grabbed two more logs from the nearby bin, and tossed them onto the flame. Then he took the poker and prodded at the old logs until they broke apart, releasing a hue of a molten center that would hopefully ignite the fresh logs. He grabbed the tongs and shifted the wood into place, then went back to sleep, hoping another nightmare wouldn't ensue.

———

THE MORNING COULDN'T HAVE COME FASTER. Miles was the last to wake, his ears being bombarded with the whistling screams of a kettle over a fire. He lifted his head from the thin pillow to find Alice still snuggled up on the couch, hunched over in pain.

"Morning," he said.

Alice looked over at him and forced a smile on her lips— a smile that showed promise as if she were the picture of health, even though the dark circles surrounding her eyes and pale skin told a different story. Alice hadn't slept well. Didn't feel well, either. She was dying, after all, and she knew it. The throbbing pain in her side worsened, and she clutched her abdomen even tighter. She couldn't even get the words out to respond to him.

"She's been runnin' a fever all morning," Katherine said, entering the living room holding a cup of ginger tea. "You think it's the food?" She held the cup up to Alice's lips and waited for her to take a sip.

"I have no clue." Miles lied.

He knew exactly what was causing her pain and discoloration. She was dying from the inside out, her organs slowly eating themselves into oblivion.

Katherine shot him a look of sincerity. "I ain't got no meds here. Nothing that can help her at least." She placed the cup down on the square oak coffee table and stepped over to the kitchen, signaling Miles to follow. She pulled him to the side. "There anythin' you wanna tell me? 'Cause I know when someone's bullshittin' me."

The jig was up. Katherine clearly knew something was wrong with Alice. There was no sense in lying anymore.

"Okay, I'll tell you, but you gotta promise me something first."

Katherine raised a brow and crossed her arms. "I don't make promises, boy. Now go on, spill it."

Miles exhaled deeply before explaining all the events that had transpired over the last four days. He was finally able to relax his tense shoulders. The stress he had been carrying had weighed heavy on him; affecting his appetite, his mood, hell even his sleep.

"I'm sorry I lied. She's just... she's just all I have left. I lost my mother to the virus and it took a week before she turned. I just assumed it'd be the same for Alice—for everyone."

Katherine was at a loss for words from the atomic truth

bomb he had dropped on her. But she didn't react how he had expected her to. She left the kitchen and plopped back down in the recliner, then gave Alice a wondrous stare. Could she really carry the virus inside her body for about a week's time? Was the virus just an overly pungent flu-like sickness? Could it be treatable? No one knew.

Then Katherine examined them both and considered how two teenagers could attempt such a journey. She even took note of how frail Miles's frame was compared to many other kids she had seen over the years. He must have loved her so to risk not only her life but his own to save her. Alice hissed as the pain radiated across her stomach. There was nothing anyone could do. Katherine stood from her chair and opened the blinds, allowing the bright sun to shine in.

Miles peered out the window and saw the snow had stopped, but not before leaving a hefty six inches on the ground. *Shit. How are we gonna make it to California now?* He glanced at Alice as she huddled into a ball from the pain, looking as if she were about to curl up and die. He managed to catch a glimpse of the sadness and uncertainty in her eyes. He needed some time to think. Some time alone.

He turned to Katherine. "I'm going for a walk. Can I trust Alice will be safe in your presence?"

Katherine nodded. "There's a jacket in that closet." She motioned to the short door under the staircase. "Take it. It's chilly out there."

Miles sifted through the closet until he found an old, heavy, leather jacket. He wrapped himself in it, then stepped outside. With his hands tucked in his pockets, he followed the wraparound front porch to the end and to the back of the house, then stopped.

How can I save her now that this snow's here? He stepped off the back porch and kicked at the fluffy snow. *I can't give up. But there's no way I can get her there in time.* Then an idea popped into his head. *Katherine must have a vehicle around here somewhere. In fact, with this being a farm, she should have a truck. Maybe she'll let us use it.*

Miles headed back toward the front of the house, poking his head in a window to see if Katherine had kept her word in not disposing of Alice. There was Alice, still lying on the couch, tossing and turning in utter pain. Satisfied that she was at least still alive, he returned to the backyard.

Wandering further into the snow, trekking through the white fluff, he spotted a large wooden barn that looked as if it were on the brink of collapse. Yet despite the amount of snow covering its roof, it still stood proud and strong. He decided to approach the building behind the house in hopes of finding a vehicle inside. When he finally managed to open one of the large wooden doors, he found more than he had expected. A spark had reignited his dulling flame.

Not only did he find a truck—a 1968 International Harvester—but next to it, under a large tarp, stood what looked like a small aircraft.

The woman who he thought would've murdered them both in cold blood after becoming aware of the truth could possibly help get them to their destination—and on time for that matter.

Miles approached the vessel and yanked off the plastic tarp, revealing a white airplane. The decal on the side read: Cessna 172 Skyhawk.

His eyes bubbled. *Man, I hope this thing runs.*

4

RECONCILIATION

M iles marched back into the house, his head held high. "Katherine?" he called out.

She came out from the kitchen, a plate, and dishtowel in her hand.

"*Please* tell me that plane out there still flies."

After receiving help from Beck in getting a vehicle, Miles believed he wouldn't need help from anyone else. But upon experiencing the recent setbacks, he quickly realized that he was in dire need of assistance once again.

"Sure does."

Miles exhaled a sigh of relief, thankful to hear that their ticket out of Portland was actually possible. But then came the next problem. Could he bear to ask the question?

"Is there any way you can fly us to California?" he asked.

Everything was riding on that one answer. If Katherine were to say yes to his request, then Miles would be able to finish his journey. But if her answer was no, then his efforts to save Alice would come to end.

"Sorry, but that ain't gon' happen, hon."

Dammit. "Can you at least give a reason why you won't?" He leaned against the stair rail, disappointment on his face.

"It's simple, Miles. Why leave this place when I have everythin' I need right here? There are so many unknowns out there. So many bad things that can happen."

"I get that, but can't you make an exception?"

Katherine shot him a *seriously* look.

"I don't get it. You've had this plane and yet you're still here. Why not leave? Fly somewhere far away and escape this place. I heard only America has been affected by the virus, not the entire world."

"You really think this place is all that bad, huh?" Katherine returned to the kitchen, Miles following after her. "I have nowhere to go, hon. I reckon there's no better place to be than here—my home."

Miles didn't fully understand what Katherine meant by having nowhere to go. She could have traveled anywhere to her heart's desire. The possibilities were endless, especially now, with a large chunk of the human population having been wiped out. Why not leave? See the places you hadn't seen before. Yeah, fuel and food were of concern, but that was it.

"But—"

"No more. I'm done talkin' 'bout it."

When begging didn't work, Miles turned to brute force.

He ventured back out into the living area—leaving Katherine to finish the dishes—where he spotted her rifle beside her recliner. He gulped and exhaled. *I don't wanna, but I gotta do something*. He grabbed the gun.

And as he did, Katherine said, "I hope you know how to use one of those."

Miles gasped as he froze, his grip tightening around the weapon. He spun around and pointed it at the woman. "Look, I don't wanna do this, but you've left me no choice."

Katherine didn't quake for one second, her hands remaining by her side. She was cool, calm, and collected—unlike Miles, his body beginning to sweat.

"You don't wanna do this," she said.

"Yes, I do," he shot back. "I've come this far to save my girlfriend, and I won't let some snow, or you, get in the way of that."

"Okay, then. Go head... shoot me." She inched closer.

"Don't!" Miles wiped the sweat from his brow.

"You do realize, if you shoot me, you're still gon' be stuck unless you know how to fly. Which from the looks of it, you don't."

Katherine got even closer to Miles, slowly reaching for the gun in his hands. She lowered the rifle, sending Miles to drop it. He began to cry.

"I'm sorry... I just... I can't lose anyone else," he managed to get out through tears.

"There, there," Katherine said, cradling him in her bosom. "No need to cry, hon. We've all lost someone we love."

"But it's all my fault she got bit. And I'm just trying to do my best to make it better." He stared into Katherine's deep brown eyes. "Please, I'm begging you. Please fly us to California."

The amount of effort—of love—a kid like Miles was willing to put in to save someone other than himself endeared him to Katherine. She softened.

"Okay," she said. "If I have the fuel, I'll fly you and your girlfriend to California."

Miles smiled. "Thank you, so much. You don't know what this means to me—to us."

––––––––

"YOU BETTER PUT your back into it," Katherine yelled to Miles as she hooked her side of the plow onto the back of her Ford 5000 tractor.

Jesus Christ, this lady's ridiculous! This thing weighs a ton! How'd she manage this by herself?

Time was running out, and they were still snowed in. If they were to make it to Alameda by nightfall, they'd need to clear the field of snow to use as a runway. As of right now, it was just the two of them. Alice was of no help. They both had been steadily preparing the tractor and plane inside the barn for about an hour now, kicking aside all the unnecessary junk she had lying around and cleaning out the plethora of boxes of machine parts that were spread about the backseat of the Skyhawk.

Miles knew once they started the tractor all hell would

break loose. Because of the sounds that the machine omitted, they'd only have so much time before whatever monsters were nearby would come to pay them a visit. Miles loaded a large container of water into the plane while Katherine checked its fluids.

"So how long have you been a pilot?" He remembered the family photos he'd seen hanging on the walls. One, in particular, showed Katherine standing beside a plane in an air force uniform.

"Fifty-two years." She topped off the oil in the aircraft. Miles closed the passenger door as she tossed the oil rag over her shoulder, then reached for the bottle of antifreeze on the nearby counter. "Plane's almost ready."

"Wonderful!"

"Got any other questions?" Katherine asked, inhaling mother nature's wonderful winter scent, the icy cold tickling the hairs in her nose.

Miles shook his head.

"Alrighty then. Grab Alice and my gun and get settled in the plane. I'm gon' start the tractor in five."

Miles darted back to the house to collect the things he and Katherine had gathered for the trip. Alice was curled up on the sofa in a deep slumber when Miles came back to get her. She didn't even squirm or feel warm when he pressed his hand to her forehead. As much as he hated disturbing what appeared to be the best sleep Alice had had in a while, Miles knew the time was now or never to leave.

"Alice? It's time to go," he whispered in her ear.

She lifted her head slightly. "What... what are you talking about?"

He heard the tractor start. "We gotta go, now."

Alice didn't want to leave the comfortable cushions she rested on—didn't even want to open her eyes or sit up, frankly, fearing the pain in her stomach might return. But Miles forced her onto her feet, wrapping the blanket around her and draping her arm around his neck, and guiding her out the back door.

When Alice spotted the small aircraft in the barn, she, too, was awestruck. Miles helped her into the tiny, cramped backseat of the aircraft as Katherine drove the tractor down the dirt path, slowly clearing a way for them to leave Oregon.

As Alice tried her best to settle into the plane, Miles stood watch, making sure nothing or no one came crawling out of the surrounding woods. He had grabbed a baseball bat he found in the corner of the barn to use to protect the plane and Katherine against any monsters that might appear. It was nothing like his first bat, but it would do. He had to protect Katherine at all costs. He had to guarantee she would make it back to the aircraft in one piece because he didn't know a thing about flying, nor did Alice.

Twenty-five minutes later, the rugged runway was finished. Miles quickly attached the hefty rope tied around the front landing gear of the plane to the plow on the tractor, and he marveled at the sight as Katherine towed it out of the barn.

As Katherine parked the tractor to the side and hopped

off, she spotted movement in the distance down the field. She squinted to try to bring the faraway image into focus.

"We've got company!" she shouted.

Miles glanced in the direction she pointed toward, but what he found wasn't what he had expected. There was no horde; no undead whatsoever. Instead, a militant group made their way up the hill in a Jeep. Perhaps they'd heard the tractor or seen the clouds of smoke coming from the house's chimney; whatever it was, they'd done something to draw unwanted attention.

"Hurry! Let's get out of here!" Keeping his bat tucked in his elbow, Miles untied the rope from the front wheel and jumped in the passenger seat, strapping himself into the safety harness. Katherine, too, rushed to the cockpit and got inside. They both put on a set of headphones that rested on the yokes. She quickly turned the ignition, started the plane, and adjusted the fuel mixture control knob until the engine came to a comfortable idle. From there she adjusted the throttle enough for the aircraft to move under its own power. They taxied through the light snow onto the dirt road, settling into a tense silence while Katherine concentrated on every move. Both of them were acutely aware that they only had one chance to get this right.

The Jeep was quickly approaching. A few shots rang out as Katherine increased the throttle speed, lunging the aircraft forward down the runway. Behind them, the Jeep plowed through the snowy hills, across the yard, past the house, and picked up speed on the cleared dirt path.

"Those your neighbors?" Miles asked, trying to break the tension.

"I've seen 'em before, unfortunately." Katherine's eyes didn't budge from the snowy dirt road. "Last time I saw 'em, they were killing friendlies left and right."

Friendlies? Miles didn't fully understand what she meant by friendlies. Civilians maybe? People who weren't affected by the virus? People who were just like him, Alice, and Katherine, trying to survive in a doomed world. But now wasn't the best time to think about that.

The aircraft was steadily increasing in speed, achieving optimum thrust for takeoff. "Pull back on that as hard as you can on my say." Katherine motioned to the yoke in front of Miles. He grabbed the contraption and got ready.

"Three, two, one... pull!"

They both pulled with all their might, sending the plane upward toward the sky. The nose of the Skyhawk lifted from the ground as the Jeep closed in. More shots rang out, missing the plane entirely until one bullet caught one of the tires on the landing gear. Katherine peered out the window, witnessing the tire flap in the wind, then separate from the rim and crash to the ground.

"Dammit!" Katherine was livid. "We just lost part of our landing gear."

Miles went into a panic, his eyes widening and his heart rate increasing as the plane continued climbing.

When the plane reached an optimum altitude and evened out, Miles finally spoke. "I guess this is it, huh? The end of the line. There's no way we're gonna be able to land this thing, is there?"

Katherine scoffed. "This ain't the first time somethin' like this has happened. I'm gon' get y'all there in one piece, don't you fret. I didn't fly fifty-two years for nothin'.'"

Miles peered out the window and admired the clouds suspended above the large squares of snow-covered farm fields below. Even though he was very concerned about how they were going to land once they arrived in Alameda, somehow the scenic view from above and Katherine's reassuring words calmed his nerves.

He had never been in a plane before, let alone been a copilot. The feeling of almost achieving his goal of saving the love of his life brought on a feeling he had never felt before. A sense of confidence. Achievement. Power.

25

The flight was rough, shuddering most of the way as the plane battled turbulence. But that wasn't what had Katherine on edge. It was the fact they barely had enough fuel to make it to their destination. She had nothing in the barn to fuel up the aircraft with before they left. She knew just how much was needed to make the 530-odd-air-mile trip. But would they make it there? She wasn't certain, but she'd be damned if she were to trouble Miles with more worry.

Plus, she was unsure if both Miles and Alice would want to return to Oregon after all was said and done if for whatever reason they arrived in Alameda and there was no cure. Especially, after cutting it close with those people in the Jeep. Just thinking about returning home made her shudder. Her place was probably in shambles now—raided and burned to the ground. What a shame.

Katherine didn't know how long it would take to get

there, but by looking at the map, it wasn't going to be much longer. They had already been flying for over an hour. She imagined it would be time for them to begin their descent shortly.

She turned on her air-band radio hoping to make contact with the naval base. The line was silent. She and Miles exchanged a quick glance before trying again. Once more she received no reply. This wasn't a good sign. The kid claimed an officer from Kitsap had spoken with someone from USCG less than a week ago. Why weren't they responding? She prayed they hadn't fallen victim to the virus like the rest of the country had.

Katherine took the initiative and began to descend into military airspace, hoping they wouldn't get shot down. "Hope y'all are ready. 'Cause, there's no clue what's gon' be waiting for us down there."

Miles clenched the handle of the baseball bat next to him. *I'm ready. No matter what happens, I'm gonna take care of you.* He peered back at Alice, who was fast asleep. Her skin looked paler than ever, and it was only the fourth day. Something told him she wasn't going to make it to Day 7. Luckily, they weren't going to need the whole week to get to Alameda. All they had to do now was find the cure.

"Grab the wheel," Katherine said to Miles, pulling back on the throttle to lower the RPMs further.

Miles grabbed ahold of the yoke and waited for further instruction. He watched the ant-like buildings and cars grow in size as Katherine guided the plane toward the runway. As they approached, she continued to decrease the plane's engine speed. The steering got heavy as the wind current tried to knock them off course, but Katherine adeptly kept control. Miles smiled. He and Alice were in good hands.

That smile was to be short-lived, however.

Boom!

An explosion sent smoke and flames rising from the ground below.

Katherine gasped. "Sweet baby Jesus!"

A blazing fire covered a corner of the base. One of the buildings had been razed to the ground. Miles trembled in his seat and struggled to collect himself. Katherine redirected his attention with an abrupt snap of her fingers in front of his face.

"On my say, push forward. Got it?"

"Got it."

As they continued their descent toward the runway, she noticed a bunch of military-grade vehicles and jets spread about the tarmac. Luckily none were in their landing path because Katherine knew if they had to reapproach, it would be all over for them. The low-fuel light had begun to flash; they wouldn't have enough fuel to circle around and try again.

Just before they touched down, Miles spotted a small horde of Silent Ones wandering around the tarmac. "Some welcome wagon," he muttered.

They crossed the first piece of pavement, decapitating one of the undead that stood at the start of it. The remaining wheels of the Skyhawk barely touched the ground. The plane bumped, then rose again.

"Push!" Katherine yelled.

They both pushed the yokes in, setting two wheels and one empty rim down onto the tarmac. The rim scraped against the asphalt, sending sparks flying from under the cockpit. Katherine brought the throttle to idle speed, cutting all fuel to the engine. They were quickly running out of runway. Miles quietly prayed to himself, hoping they wouldn't crash through the steel fence that was rapidly approaching.

The Skyhawk cruised off the tarmac and into some grass, finally slowing to a stop a few yards away from the fence line.

"Phew, that was close," Miles said.

Katherine looked at Miles as though everything had gone exactly as planned. "Said I'd get y'all here, didn't I?"

"That you did."

———

"HERE THEY COME!" Katherine yelled, drawing her Winchester and aiming it at some ungodly creature about thirty yards out.

Miles pulled Alice from the backseat and carried her in his arms, leaving behind the baseball bat he had brought with him from the farm. Katherine let off one round as Miles made his way to the nearest building. He ran across the tarmac onto a sidewalk, and Katherine was quick to follow.

Miles glanced down at an almost unconscious Alice in

his arms. *I'm gonna save your life if it's the last thing I do.* When he looked back up, he spotted a few of the Silent Ones nearby; they were stumbling their way past a wrecked helicopter and heading his way.

"Shit," he muttered under his breath.

Being outside was unsafe. There were too many variables in the environment. He quickly checked his surroundings. Finding a window nearby, he peered in only to find more of the undead inside. *This doesn't look good.* He shuddered.

"Over here," Katherine yelled. She opened a door and disappeared into the dimly lit building, leaving the door ajar.

Miles rushed over and followed her in, hoping her choice of shelter was advantageous. As soon as he entered, Katherine slammed the door behind him, shutting out the two monsters that had been closing in on him.

The piercing sound of metal on metal echoed down the empty hallway. The fluorescent tubes in the ceiling flickered endlessly. From a quick glance, the place looked to be a medical facility. Gurneys and IV poles were strewn across the hallway, and the floor was covered in a mix of scattered paper and blood. They carefully crept down the hall, making sure to keep an eye out for anyone or anything that looked to be abnormal. As they passed empty room after empty room, dead body after dead body, Miles stared through the window of a closed door to find the same two Silent Ones he had spotted earlier when he peeked in through the window from outside.

Miles let out a deep sigh. *What happened here?* Something didn't seem right. *How could USCG have gone from fully operational to a deserted crypt within just a few days?* Something was up. *Could the surviving personnel have relocated to another location? Or is everyone dead?* He hoped it wasn't the latter.

They turned a corner into another corridor, where they encountered a few more bodies—all navy men with gunshots to their heads. Blood covered the white-painted cinderblock walls and the once-shiny tiled floor. It was a shit show—and one made by a living, breathing human, apparently, since as far as Miles knew, the undead couldn't shoot guns.

Miles couldn't shake the feeling that the place had been like this for months. Empty. Deserted. The extent of decay of the dead bodies, and the horrid stench in the air, provided strong testimony that it had been like this for at least a few weeks. *Maybe I should've spoken to them over the radio before leaving.*

Katherine opened the door to the stairwell and held it open for Miles to pass through. At this point, they had given up looking for a miracle cure for the virus; they were simply searching for any signs of life.

As they traveled up the first flight to the second floor, they encountered something blocking the staircase that prevented them from going any further. Katherine carefully opened the door to the hallway and poked her head out, gasped, and immediately pulled her head back into the stairwell, closing the door softly behind her.

"What is it?" Miles whispered.

She sighed. "They're everywhere. No way anyone's alive in there."

Miles lowered his head in dismay. *Fuck.* At this point, it was either knuckle down or give up, and he wasn't about giving up, especially now that they had come this far. It was at that moment that Alice mustered up enough energy to say something.

"Their blood." Miles leaned his head in closer to her mouth to hear her faint words. "They smell... our blood."

Maybe Alice was onto something. Miles thought back to the man who pulled the tattered woman behind him. She wasn't chasing after the man, just following him, like a dog on a leash. That man was covered in blood. But who's blood? The only feasible answer he could come up with was the blood of the undead.

"Quick, let's cover ourselves in their blood."

"What?" Katherine shot back.

"Somehow, someway they can smell us. So if we cover ourselves in their blood, I think we can sneak by them undetected."

"You sure that'll work?"

"No. But it's worth a shot." Miles gently placed Alice down on the steps of the staircase and hurried back down to the first floor, where he ventured back out into the hallway. He looked over the dead bodies they'd encountered there until one, in particular, caught his eye. It had been brutally battered with bullet holes, its stomach disemboweled. Its face showed signs of age, making it far from a fresh kill.

"You sure you wanna do this?" Katherine had come up behind him.

"Right now, it doesn't look like we have much of a choice."

Taking a deep breath, Miles reached into the open abdomen of the monster he so desperately despised, sliding his hands deep under the lower intestines. The organs were slimy and thick like pudding. He tried his best not to gag as he pulled his hand out and rubbed the blood over his face and forearms. He knew it was going to take more than just a few drops to fully mask the smell of his oxygenated blood with the awful stench of the undead, so he decided to undress. He shed his shirt and rolled up his pant legs to get the best amount of coverage, then dove in for more.

Katherine watched in horror as Miles doused himself in the thick, dark liquid. She was hesitant to do so, but like Miles, she didn't want to die. She got down on one knee and began to roll up her pant legs, then took off her flannel. She rubbed the blood against her skin, slathering it on as if she were a pig playing in the mud.

"It's only temporary," Miles said.

Afterward, they quickly redressed, then slowly made their way back upstairs, where Miles rubbed as much blood as he could on Alice. When they were all covered, Katherine slowly opened the door, Miles picked up Alice, and they ventured onto the second floor.

The scene was horrifying. Bodies upon bodies were spread about the linoleum. The remaining undead were in huddles, feasting upon the remains of soldiers and scientists alike. The halls reverberated the munching and squishing sounds that came from flesh and tendons being torn and ripped from the bones and bellies of the deceased.

As they snuck down the hall, tiptoeing by every monster—acting as if they were monsters themselves—they were stunned when they heard a voice cry out. Miles glanced down to find a man staring up at him. The left side of his abdomen was missing, and he was pleading to be put out of his misery.

But there was nothing Miles could do. He had no weapon. Not a gun nor a knife to help the man. Even if he had, it wouldn't be a smart idea to perform such an act of humanity while trying to play the role of the monster. It would only lead to more problems. So Miles averted his eyes and continued onward, shame and regret stirring in his stomach.

It seemed to take an eternity, but eventually, the trio made it down the hallway to the door that led to the emergency stairwell on the other end of the second floor. Miles hoped it wasn't locked because he couldn't bear to see that scientist again—couldn't bear to turn him down for a second time. He closed his eyes as he pressed his back to the bar and breathed a quiet sigh of relief when the door opened.

Miles was holding the door open to allow Katherine to pass through into the stairwell when Alice let out a single cough. It was all it took to alert the Silent Ones nearby that there was a beating heart in their midst.

"Move!" Katherine shouted, shoving Miles into the stairwell and closing the door behind them in one brisk movement.

Miles rushed up the steps as fast as he could, hoping they wouldn't encounter any more undead on the next floor. Huffing and puffing, Katherine was right on his tail, struggling through old age to keep up. They skipped the third floor and headed straight for the fourth. They had no idea where they were going or what, exactly, they were looking for. All they had was perseverance.

When they arrived on the fourth floor, they found they'd reached the top floor of the building. The end of the line.

26

Having reached the top floor, Miles burst through the door and entered the hallway, unsure of whether he'd be faced by the living or the undead. Katherine followed, her shoes squeaking against the noticeably cleaner tile floor. As the stairwell door slammed behind them, an office door down the hallway opened, and a Korean man in a white lab coat stepped out.

"We need help!" Miles called out. "Please, can you help us?"

The man nodded, waving them into the room. Once they were all inside the office, he locked the door behind them.

"Is it just you three?" he asked.

"Unfortunately," Katherine answered.

"What happened here?" Miles asked, looking around the room. Everything around him seemed unaffected by the bloodbath the floors below had experienced.

"The better question is, what didn't happen?" the man asked, and the question confused Miles. He walked into the adjoining room, sat on a high stool, and spun around to face the trio. "What is it that you need assistance with?"

"My girlfriend."

He motioned for Alice to come to him so he could assess her. When Miles entered alongside her, he stopped in his tracks. What he saw frightened him. The place looked like the lair of a mad scientist—a high school laboratory filled with beakers, flasks, miscellaneous chemicals, and baby fetuses all stored in mason jars on a rack against the wall. There were even two of the undead locked in cages like animals and one spread out on another table, its rib cage split in two as if the man had been dissecting it.

Miles's stomach churned.

"Go ahead and sit on the table, here," the man said, indicating a tall counter near the stool on which he sat.

Miles put his hand on her arm to signal his hesitation. "First, you gotta tell us what's going on here. Who are you? And why are you the only one left?" His chest tightened. He was still in fight or flight mode.

The man exhaled. "My apologies. It's been a while since I've had to exchange pleasantries with living beings. I am Dr. Tae-hyung, the lead scientist here at the base. Well, I wasn't before, but I am—"

"Before what? The outbreak?" Miles interrupted.

"Yes. And after for a time. For the first three months, we were fine. The outbreak didn't affect many of us at all. And the few that did get sick, we quarantined... until they died."

Dr. Tae-hyung walked over to the nearest window and gazed down at the undead aimlessly wandering the grounds. "We tried our best to save those men back then. We were able to postpone the side effects of the virus," he bowed his head in shame, "but unfortunately, we were unsuccessful in saving them."

"But that still doesn't explain where everyone went," Miles said.

"After those men died, we continued experimenting on soldiers, trying to find a possible solution—"

"But one thing led to another and everyone got sick and started killin' each other," Katherine said, examining one of the mason jars on the shelf. "Sound 'bout right?"

Dr. Tae-hyung nodded. "And to think everything was under control just a few months ago." As if trying to recall a long-forgotten memory, he added: "And you said your names were...?"

"I'm Miles. This is Alice."

"And I'm Katherine."

Miles helped Alice onto the counter. Dr. Tae-hyung pried open each eye one at a time and saw that her pupils were dilated, and the whites of her eyes were bloodshot. "So you guys were working on an antidote when things went bad," Miles said. "But I heard from someone recently that you were close. Did you ever find one? Can you save her?"

Dr. Tae-hyung removed his prescription glasses from his face, pinched the bridge of his nose, and exhaled. "Honestly, I am unsure. It truly depends on how far the virus has progressed." He looked at Alice. "An antidote has been created, but if I give it to you, I can't guarantee you will survive."

Alice's voice was weak but determined. "If you don't give it to me, I'm guaranteed not to survive."

"We've gone through hell to get here," Miles chimed in. "There's no turning back now." The room fell quiet, and Miles, for the first time since discovering the bite mark on Alice's shoulder, began to relax. He grabbed a stool, slid it near the table, sat down, and grabbed hold of Alice's hand.

"She got bit, and it's all my fault," he admitted, bowing his head over her body. "I should've never hesitated with that gun."

"Some things in life are out of our control," Dr. Tae-hyung said, checking Alice's vitals. "Sometimes the only thing we can do is take what life hands us and make the best of the situation. To be honest, before you guys arrived, I wasn't so sure if I would make it out of here. But taking into account what has transpired over the past three months, I now know the possibilities are endless."

Sharing a moment of silence, Dr. Tae-hyung ventured over to the whiteboard and studied what notes he'd written. "From what information I have gathered over the past few months, every subject experiences the same initial reaction from the virus. Intense fatigue, vomiting, diarrhea, headaches, and even seizures. What I have found is that there are three stages to the disease. Vital organs begin to fail in the second stage. Subjects with a strong enough immune system can fend off the disease longer than others, giving them an increased chance of survival, pushing organ failure into the third stage."

"But what's that gots to do with the antidote?" Katherine asked.

"Well, it helps us determine who has a better chance at recovering and who doesn't. Look at it this way," he picked up a vial of dark-green liquid from the counter and pointed to it. "Hypothetically speaking, say this is the cure, and I inject Alice with it. If she were in the third stage, then even after the virus has been completely eliminated from her body, her organs would still be beyond repair. She would be destined to live the rest of her life on dialysis." Then to Miles, he added: "How many days has it been since she got bit?"

Miles had to recount the days on his fingers as his memory was shot from the lack of sleep over the past week. "Four days... I think."

The doctor turned back to Alice. "Well, you are young, and you look like you were healthy before the bite. If his calculations are correct, and if you are lucky enough to have a strong immune system, then I believe you are just beginning the third stage." Three faces looked at the doctor with hopeful anticipation. "There is a moderate probability the antidote will give you more time. There is a small probability that it will allow you to recover entirely."

———

"I SEE you guys have come a long way," Dr. Tae-hyung said, trekking down the hall as Miles and Katherine followed.

"Sure did," Miles said. "All the way from Seattle."

"Not me," Katherine added. "I'm comin' from Portland, but I was born and raised in Alabama."

Dr. Tae-hyung took a right at the end of the hall, then ventured into another room labeled PHARMACY. He grabbed a few items from a glass cabinet. "Here, hold these." He handed Miles some sealed packets, then went for the fridge to grab a blood bag. "By any chance, do you know what her blood type is?"

Miles shook his head. "No, sorry."

"No need to apologize. I'll just grab some O negative then." Dr. Tae-hyung relocked the fridge and supply cabinet, then headed for the door. A minute later they returned to the room where now Alice lay fast asleep on the counter. The adrenaline that had propelled her through the nightmare of the trek from Seattle to the naval base had left her body, and she had succumbed to her exhaustion.

After laying out the medical supplies and bag of blood on the counter, Dr. Tae-hyung helped Miles clean the foreign blood from Alice's body, clearing the crevice between her forearm and bicep for transfusion. Then he wrapped a tourniquet around her limb and inserted a needle.

"She is extremely dehydrated. Because of this, she will need some time before I give her the antidote. After the saline and the blood, she should be ready. In the meantime, there is a bathroom down the hall. You two can clean up there if you would like. I will be in the lab." He left the room.

"He sounds Korean," Katherine noted, lifting Alice gently from the table to help Miles clean the blood from her back.

"Makes sense." Miles grabbed a fresh box of wipes from the windowsill. "The same day I heard about this place possibly creating a cure, I also heard that South Korea was the only country willing to help us. Maybe they brought him over here to help in the labs."

"Hmm, maybe."

After he cleaned Alice up, Miles examined her wound. It had scabbed over, but it showed clear signs of infection. The surrounding skin had turned bright red, and the surrounding veins had blackened as if they were already dead.

You're gonna pull through this Alice. I know you will.

———

THREE HOURS PASSED before Dr. Tae-hyung strolled back into the room with the antidote in hand.

"Think she's ready for the antidote now?" Miles asked, hoping it wasn't too late.

"Let's take a look." Dr. Tae-hyung walked over to Alice, inspected how much blood had been transfused, and took her vitals. Miles couldn't breathe as he awaited the doctor's assessment.

"We can proceed."

Miles wasn't sure he'd ever heard three more beautiful words spoken. He watched as the doctor injected a syringe into the IV line, administering the antidote.

"It looks like I've done my job," Katherine said, perched on the windowsill.

"And I thank you for that," Miles said. Then to Dr. Tae-hyung, he added: "So what now? How long before we know if it worked?"

Dr. Tae-hyung removed the saline pouch and disposed of it along with the empty syringe. "Her body should begin to show signs of improvement within a few hours. But as for her recovery, it depends on her immune system and how well equipped it is to defeat the virus."

Katherine exhaled. "Well, the way I see it, looks like we've got nothin' but time." She scratched at her stomach. "There any food here? 'Cause I'm gettin' hungry."

"Yes, there is," Dr. Tae-hyung answered. "There is a vending machine down on the first floor. You probably passed it on your way up. Take the stairwell on the South-side of the building, the other one is blocked."

Katherine headed for the door. "Thanks."

As Katherine left to go calm her hunger pains, curiosity still lingered within Miles. *Why is Dr. Tae-hyung the only person left in the building?* Dr. Tae-hyung approached the whiteboard and started erasing the three formulas for the concoctions that didn't work after circling the one that did. He selected a notebook from the shelf and copied it down.

As Miles took a seat back on the stool he said, "I can't thank you enough for saving Alice."

"Don't thank me yet. She is not in the clear. Though, the antidote will eliminate the virus, the status of her organs is the true determining factor on whether she will survive."

Miles bowed his head in understanding. "Okay, well, thank you for trying at least." In the awkward silence that followed his gratefulness, Miles wondered if he should raise his question once again. Why Dr. Tae-hyung was the only one left? As the doctor continued writing in his notebook, Miles caved. "You know, you never answered my question on what happened here." Dr. Tae-hyung stopped writing and turned to Miles. "How did everyone die and not—"

"Me," Dr. Tae-hyung said bluntly. He cleared his throat. "It may be hard to believe, but I am—how you say?—lucky." He joked.

Before Miles could question the doctor some more, Alice started coughing, breaking his train of thought. "We should sit her up," the doctor ordered.

Dr. Tae-hyung and Miles moved Alice to a seated position, then the doctor quickly checked on Alice using the stethoscope wrapped around his neck. When he didn't find anything abnormal in her breathing, he said, "I have seen this before. It should pass shortly." Then, an alarm buzzed on his wristwatch. Tapping the button to silence it, he announced, "I will be right back." He darted out of the room, tending to something of greater importance.

What did he feel was more important than Alice at that moment that needed to be addressed? Miles didn't know. But he quickly brought his attention back to Alice, reaching for her hand to show he was present. He patiently waited by her side, praying, and hoping. But when her coughing spell didn't end, he grew anxious. Then he remembered what Dr. Tae-hyung had said. *"I'll be right back."*

Why would he say that? How could a doctor just leave his patient in her time of need like that?

Miles quickly released Alice's hand and raced out of the room and down the hall in search of the scientist. After a minute of checking other rooms, he found him. He was in a room labeled LABORATORY. The door had been left ajar. Before Miles entered, he overheard the doctor talking to someone. But who? He wished he could hear exactly what was being said, but the voices were too muffled to make out.

He gently knocked on the door, then pushed it open. "She's still coughing," he yelled. "Come quick!"

Dr. Tae-hyung quickly turned off his computer monitor, shot up from his desk, and went for the door as Katherine shouted for help from down the hall. When they both returned to the room, they found Alice fully conscious, but in bad shape. Her breathing was heavy and sluggish, her heart was racing, she had a high fever, and she had vomited onto the floor. But what was most unsettling was that her vomit was completely red as if it were blood, not stomach acid.

Dr. Tae-hyung went for the AKG monitor in the corner of the room and attached it to Alice with a pulse oximeter. After gathering some information on her vitals, he could tell the antidote was working. Her body had reacted in a way he had never seen before. This was not a surprise to Dr. Tae-hyung given that the antidote was so new, so he remained confident that Alice was progressing well despite what looked like a setback.

"The antidote is doing its job," he said. "As of right now, her fever is my only concern. I will give her something to lower it. But that is all I can do."

"Is there any chance she'll get worse?" Miles asked.

Dr. Tae-hyung inhaled deeply, tucking his hands into the pockets of his lab coat. "Unfortunately, I don't know. Only time will tell." He left the room to retrieve the medication Alice needed.

With the doctor gone, Miles crossed his arms and leaned against the counter on which Alice lay. In a low tone, he said, "There's something off about this guy. I overheard him talking to someone in the lab, I just don't know who or what about."

Katherine nodded. "I'll take a look 'round, see if I find anythin'. You just focus on her, okay?"

Turning to Alice he said, "Okay." He tucked her hair behind her ear and she smiled weakly.

When Dr. Tae-hyung returned, he had a glass of water, a pill, and a container in his hands. He handed Alice the fever reducer, and she took it with a sip of water. "That should do the trick." Then he knelt down next to the red substance on the floor and took a sample. Leaving the room, he stopped in the doorway and turned to Miles. "If she gets worse, let me know. I will be in the lab." He left the room, disappearing again down the hall.

We finally made it. We finally made it to California. Within four days, too! I wasn't sure how much longer Alice would've been able to hold on. She was starting to lose consciousness more often, and it didn't seem like she had much time left. If it weren't for Katherine I don't know what I'd have done. God, I'm so thankful I was able to save Alice. Granted, she's not in the clear just yet, but still. She's on the road to recovery.

Hopefully, she gets better. No, when she gets better. Now that I think about it, I haven't thought about where we're gonna go once she's fully healed. We could go back to the compound, but there's no guarantee they'll let us in. To think of it, I don't know if we can even make it back to Seattle. Especially with the plane like it is. Maybe we should venture further inland to see if we can find any other survivors. That might work.

Sincerely, M.W.

27

Hours passed as the sun reached its peak and disappeared once more. It had been eight hours since they had arrived at the naval base; five since Alice was given the antidote. She was getting better now. Her color had returned along with her consciousness. Even her hunger came back, so Miles's thoughts turned to fetch them both food for the evening.

It was 7 P.M. when his stomach started to growl heavily. He had learned to suppress his appetite early on in the apocalypse with the help of fasting, but his old habits were starting to resurface now that he had given his body more food than he needed back at the compound. And eating the venison Katherine had prepared the previous day only made it worse. His body craved sustenance, as did Alice's.

"Did you bring us any food?" Miles asked Katherine, seeing her munch on a bag of pretzels, assuming she had emptied the entire machine to share among them.

"I didn't," she said. "But there's some peanuts and M&Ms left."

Miles sighed. It wasn't much, but it would have to do. "I'll be right back."

He left the room and walked down the hall toward the south stairwell. Uneasiness lingered in the back of his mind as he roamed the premises without a weapon in fear that at any moment he could be attacked by the Silent Ones. But upon witnessing Katherine make it back in one piece, he took the risk. The stairwell was dimly lit and smelly, carrying a stench of disemboweled body parts of forgotten soldiers. Continuing to creep down the steps, one floor after another, he had a realization. A moment of gratitude.

I can't believe I got her here in one piece. Some awful things happened along the way, that's for sure, but we made it, and she's okay. I'm just thankful we're both still alive. Thankful that I was able to conquer my anxiety. Well sort of. I'm also glad I got a chance to ride a motorcycle, too. God, I hope we make it outta here together.

Miles stepped out onto the first floor and approached the vending machine to find its face had been punched in, leaving remnants of glass to lay in front of it all over the tiled floor. He laughed internally. *I guess vandalism isn't a big deal in the apocalypse.* He assumed Katherine was responsible, maybe even the doctor, but felt it'd be best not to mention it. He quickly grabbed what he needed and headed back upstairs.

When Miles returned to the room, he found Dr. Taehyung running more tests on Alice. He was rechecking her vitals, then took some blood samples to analyze in the lab. The amount of blood he took from Alice alarmed Miles enough that he was tempted to say something about it, but he didn't. He just handed Alice a bag of peanuts and hoped it would be enough to aid in her blood regenerating process.

"Is there anything I can help with?" he asked Dr. Tae-hyung, opening the bag of M&Ms in his hand.

"No," Dr. Tae-hyung snarled. "The process of carrying out these tests is quite cumbersome. Plus you have to be meticulous during the testing process or else you could waste samples. And there is no time for that."

His answer confirmed Miles's suspicions. He glanced at Katherine as the doctor left the room to return to the lab. She nodded, waited a moment to ensure she wouldn't be seen, then left the room.

————

KATHERINE QUIETLY STEPPED out into the hallway. Dr. Tae-hyung had already turned the corner when she started down the hall, tiptoeing behind the sounds of his footsteps. She snuck around the corner and approached the laboratory. There she heard Dr. Tae-hyung doing what Miles said he had caught him doing earlier. But this time the door was closed.

Attempting to see who he was talking to, she peered into the room through the rectangular window on the door. The doctor was engaged in a face-to-face satellite transmission with someone dressed in a high-ranking military uniform.

She caught her breath, covering her hand over her mouth. She quickly dropped to one knee and pressed her ear against the solid wooden door. She strained to hear their conversation and quickly realized it wouldn't matter if she heard it clear as a bell; the two were speaking Korean.

For two minutes straight Katherine couldn't decipher a single word. It wasn't until the end of the conversation that she managed to hear something she remembered from her time in the Korean War. The words that were engraved in her head. *Buhkan.* Which, in English, translated to the words North Korea. She listened some more and heard the doctor sweep some papers off his desk in anger, then yell in his native tongue.

Katherine contemplated revealing her presence, but she had a feeling that in doing so she might jeopardize her safety and that of Miles and Alice. But if she were to relay what she had unearthed to Miles, he might approach the doctor and escalate the situation. As she mulled over what to do, the sound of approaching footsteps startled her.

She shot up from the floor and went to knock, but as she did the door swung open. "Oh, hey. I was just coming to talk to you 'bout something," she said nonchalantly.

"Okay, what about?" Dr. Tae-hyung crossed his arms.

"It's 'bout the kid. You know he's just tryna make sure his girlfriend gets better. He's been through a lot, you know. Cut him some slack."

"Slack," the Doctor repeated. "I know he's grateful to me and all for saving his girlfriend's life, but she is just one out of millions. What I am doing is bigger than him... bigger than all of us. If any of you knew just how many soldiers I can protect now that I've found a vaccine, then—"

"Vaccine?" Katherine questioned.

Dr. Tae-hyung had lost his temper and misspoke. Unfortunately for him, Katherine wasn't an idiot. "My mistake. I meant to say—"

"I heard you. There was no mistake in what you just said."

He pulled his glasses from his face and gave her an intimidating glare in hopes she'd back off. But when she didn't, he turned and stormed off in defeat.

"I know when someone's bullshittin' me!" Katherine yelled. The doctor disappeared into another room, leaving the door to slam as it closed.

Quickly realizing she had created a wonderful opportunity, Katherine peered back into the laboratory. She couldn't help wondering what he was actually doing here in the States, and she imagined she might find some answers inside that room. She turned the knob and opened the door, aware that she had to be quick: Dr. Tae-hyung would return at any moment. She rushed inside and went straight for the desk.

Katherine tried her best not to move anything while searching for any information that might tell her something about the doctor's mission. When her foot slipped on a piece of paper under the desk, she remembered the sound of the rustling papers just before the doctor ended his call. Maybe he dropped one and didn't notice in his rage. Katherine knelt down and grabbed it.

Bingo.

She had come across something useful. Though the document was typed in Korean, there was just enough English on the paper to provide a solid lead: PROJECT WIDOW.

———

TENSION HUNG in the air that night. Not only between Katherine and the doctor, but also within Miles. He had impatiently waited up half the night for Dr. Tae-hyung to return to the room with good news—that Alice was cured, healed, and healthy. But when Katherine returned with the news of what she'd uncovered in the laboratory, he came to believe the likelihood of that was slim.

Miles finally had fallen asleep on the windowsill, but only for about three hours before he was awoken by the glaring sun shining onto his face through the glass pane. He opened his eyes to find Dr. Tae-hyung already in the room checking Alice's vitals. He soon noticed, with some concern, that Katherine was nowhere to be found, only Alice and the doctor.

"I hope you don't plan on taking any more blood," Miles said, standing from the windowsill. "I can't imagine she has much more left after last night."

"Relax." Dr. Tae-hyung listened to her heart and lungs with the stethoscope. "I'm not taking anymore, just checking her vitals. I have all that I need."

"I do feel much better now," Alice admitted. "Just a little lightheaded."

"Good, you should. The lightheadedness is to be expected." The doctor removed the needle used for her transfusion and placed a small patch of gauze and medical tape over the puncture site. "After a few good meals, you should be back to your old self." He beamed.

"That's if you don't kill us first," Miles muttered.

"Miles!" Alice yelled. "What's gotten into you?"

"It's not me, Alice," he answered. "It's what this guy's been keeping from us." He reached in his pocket and fished out the folded piece of paper Katherine had taken from the laboratory the previous night. He held it up. "What's Project Widow?"

Dr. Tae-hyung froze. "How'd you get that?"

Miles ignored his question. "I asked you a question."

The doctor turned to Miles and scoffed—a scoff that turned into a laugh. "You read it, didn't you? Oh wait, it is in Korean. And unless you know how to read Korean, it is just a measly piece of paper."

Katherine reentered the room from her early morning stroll up on the roof to find the tension in the air quite unpleasant. Then she spotted Miles holding the paper she had uncovered. "I just spotted a copter headed this way," she reported.

The doctor's eyes grew wide. "I guess this is goodbye, everyone."

He went for the door, but Katherine blocked the exit.

"You ain't goin' nowhere," she said.

Dr. Tae-hyung slowly retreated, backing away from Katherine with his palms to the sky.

Alice stood from the table, snatched the paper from Miles's hand, and scanned it. After a few seconds, she questioned the doctor. "What is this? And why's it in Korean?"

Dr. Tae-hyung lowered his arms and looked out the window to survey the peril the city had undergone. He had been found out. But it didn't matter now; he had achieved his mission. "It was a controlled test. North Korea wanted to see how effective a virus could be on a country's population to use in military applications—"

"Biological warfare," Katherine explained, stepping away from the door.

"Exactly," the Doctor continued, placing his hands on the windowsill. "An antidote was made, but the costs of manufacturing enough doses for every soldier were too high. And the risk of them getting misplaced or damaged during combat was also a concern. So they tasked me with the job of creating a vaccine instead."

Working as an undercover agent for the South Korean government, Dr. Tae-hyung had volunteered to assist the U.S. Navy as a temporary foreign military assistant—a position created out of desperation when most of the U.S. Armed Forces succumbed to the virus—soon after the *Great Reset* began. When he arrived, he was ordered to conduct reconnaissance in the field. For the first three months, he had collected as many specimens as he could, which he used to concoct what he believed was the perfect recipe. After three months of research via trial and error, he was confident he had successfully created a vaccine. But one thing was missing—a key component to it all. A test subject.

In order for him to successfully label the vaccine a success, he'd first need to test it on someone. The thought to test it on himself lingered in his mind, but for the life of him, he couldn't do it. To come face to face with the undead, hoping he wouldn't succumb to the same demise everyone else endured after getting bit. For if the formula failed, he wouldn't live to perfect it.

"But why here?" Miles questioned. "Why America?"

"Why not?" Dr. Tae-hyung said. He turned to face them. "America is the easiest target. The way you Americans live is disgusting. Your greed, gluttony, hygiene. You did this to yourselves."

The sound of smacking wind echoed from afar. The helicopter was approaching. The doctor was smart enough not to run for the door. He needed a distraction big enough to hold the three of them off until he could escape. He lunged at the gun Katherine had left leaning up against the wall and aimed it at her. Everyone froze.

"I don't want to hurt you. Any of you." He pointed the gun at each of them in turn.

Every couple of seconds he shifted to a new target. It was clear from the way he shook, the way his finger barely rested on the trigger, that Dr. Tae-hyung had never held a gun before. They could tell he wasn't going to shoot them.

Just as Katherine was about to attempt to smack the weapon out of the doctor's grasp, he suddenly lunged toward the cage near the shelf of stored fetuses and threw the lock, allowing the Silent Ones held inside to escape.

"Shit!" Katherine yelled.

Dr. Tae-hyung tossed the gun across the room, leaped over the counter, and made a mad dash for the door, shoving Katherine out of the way as he burst through it. He ran straight to the laboratory to grab what he could of his research.

Alice clenched onto Miles in fear they'd get torn to shreds by the approaching undead. Their bodies trembled with fear.

Reaching for the closest thing that had a heavy feel, Miles launched a tray of dissecting tools at the monster. But it did nothing. As it continued to approach, Alice reached for another item, a heavy steel microscope, hoping it'd have more of an effect. She stepped toward the half-eaten man and struck him in the head over and over until his body dropped to the floor with a heavy thud. By the time she was finished, Alice was covered in blood.

At the same time that Alice dropped the blood-drenched microscope, Katherine was pulling the butt of her Winchester out of the skull of the other monster. She had managed to get ahold of her rifle by leading the monster toward the whiteboard where it had landed.

After wiping the blood from her gun onto the shirt of the undead as best she could, Katherine ran to the door to follow after Dr. Tae-hyung. Miles and Alice were close behind her.

But what they found when the door opened wasn't the peaceful and quiet floor they'd spent the last night on. The hallway was now a wasteland filled with a horde of the undead. The doctor had trapped them.

"But where did they all come from?" Alice wondered aloud.

Katherine loaded another round into the barrel of her rifle and whipped the gun up onto her shoulder. "You don't wanna know."

28

D r. Tae-hyung was in the laboratory collecting all of his research when a shot rang out. He winced at the sound. He knew he had to be quick; the chances of being killed by the people who considered him a bad guy were increasing every minute. A notification for an incoming email popped up on the desktop, giving him the signal that the chopper had landed. It was time to go.

Dr. Tae-hyung pulled a golden key from his lab coat, opened the bottom left-hand drawer of his steel desk, and retrieved the Glock 19 from inside. He didn't want to take any chances of getting shot while escaping. The cold metal felt good in his hands. A lot lighter than the rifle he'd held earlier. He quickly released the clip to inspect how many bullets it had. Reloading the gun, he cocked the weapon and went for the door.

Dr. Tae-hyung plowed through the doorway to push whatever might be on the other side out of the way. He glanced down the hall to find the others battling the monsters. He held out his gun but quickly lowered it, seeing no immediate danger. In his hesitation, Katherine turned and took a shot at him. She hit him in the hand that held his weapon, causing the doctor to drop everything.

Dr. Tae-hyung quickly picked up the briefcase with all his research in it, then turned and ran for the stairwell, clenching his hand as he ran. He used his lab coat to stop the bleeding as best he could, but it was of no use. The bullet had caught him in the crevice between his pointer finger and thumb, leaving blood to pump out with every beat of his heart. Bursting through the fire exit, he quickly propped the door open with the bar he had set up the previous night, then headed down two levels to open the door, inviting more of the undead to ascend. As soon as he opened the door, the undead began lumbering up the stairwell, following after the doctor as he ascended to the rooftop.

From there, the doctor escaped on the helicopter, leaving Miles, Alice, and Katherine for dead.

———

AS KATHERINE TRIED to fend off the Silent Ones, Miles and Alice tried their best to stay calm. They were weaponless and scared. Miles's heart raced as Alice clung to him like a newborn to its mother.

Katherine looked back. "What y'all waitin' for? Grab somethin' and start hittin' 'em!"

They crept backward, down the hall toward the stairwell until Miles almost tripped over the Glock Dr. Tae-hyung had dropped. He hesitantly picked it up and aimed it at one of the monsters, but he didn't pull the trigger. Couldn't.

Continuing to inch backward, Alice glanced over her shoulder to find more monsters were coming their way from the opposite direction. "Oh, God."

She reached for the fire extinguisher on the wall and snatched it off. Her initial thought was to pull the pin and empty the container, but she decided to use it as a blunt weapon instead. It made better sense to do so. Alice lunged at a one-armed woman and cracked her skull open. The monster dropped to the ground, causing the others behind it to stumble and fall over her. Katherine then used the butt of her rifle to smash in the tops of their heads as they tried to stand.

Miles couldn't do a thing except for watch in terror as his mind raced. *Don't get bit. Don't get bit. You can't get bit. I can't get bit.* He'd never seen so many of the undead in one place in all his time alone. It was a crippling sight. As he stood paralyzed in fear, his back against the cinderblock wall, Alice grabbed his hand and led him away from the ever-growing pack of the undead. Katherine was right behind them, but as she turned around to run, she tripped.

Crash!

She hit the floor hard and yelped. "My hip! I think it's broken!" She tried to get up but failed. The pain shot up her spine, sending her to curl into a ball.

"Shit!" Alice said. Dropping the fire extinguisher, she

rushed to Katherine's side. She wrapped her arm around the old lady and tried to lift her. She shot Miles a *what the fuck do we do?* look. "Don't just stand there, Miles. Help me!"

The Silent Ones were gaining on them. Miles dropped to one knee and grabbed Katherine's other side to help hoist her up. With Katherine now incapacitated, Miles was in a full-blown panic. His heart was racing faster than ever. He was hyperventilating. The walls were starting to close in. Yet his legs were still moving. His arms still held Katherine's weight. He was still, somehow, in control.

With Katherine under their arms, they moved down the hall as far as they could. But with the undead steadily approaching from both ends, their situation didn't look promising. They didn't have enough time to cover themselves in blood to use as camouflage, and there seemed to be no escape.

They lowered Katherine to the floor and propped her up against the wall. Within an instant, Alice was attacked by a monster. It managed to grab hold of her hair and pulled, almost taking her to the ground. One bite to the neck, and she'd be gone instantly. No amount of antidote would have made a difference if her jugular were severed. She flailed around, trying her best to free herself from the monster's grasp, but she couldn't get away.

Alice called out to Miles, her voice drenched in fear— fear that she'd never see him again, in fear they'd never be able to grow old together.

The sound knocked Miles out of his trance. Everything stopped. Time slowed. His body went numb. The colors he saw turned vivid, and a calm fell over him. It was as if he had died and gone to heaven. It was at that moment that he remembered what Alice had told him on graduation day. *"You're just overthinking things. Relax. You're moving at just the right pace."*

Relax. Miles no longer was going to allow his past trauma, fears, and anxiety to consume him. He knew exactly what he had to do. He glared down at the gun in his hand as Alice screamed his name once more. He could hear her now, whispering in his ear. *"I believe in you, Miles."*

He put two hands on the Glock and lifted the weapon. He looked down the sight and locked onto his target. An image of his father flashed before his eyes. He blinked multiple times until he saw Alice again. Then—with his finger on the trigger—he inhaled deeply.

I'm sorry, Dad. A tear rolled down his cheek as he pulled the trigger. The bullet entered the eye of the man that had a hold on the love of his life, then exited out the back of his skull, penetrating another monster that stood behind him. His grasp on Alice released, and his body dropped to the floor with a thud.

Miles didn't know how many more rounds were left in the clip. He just knew if they were going to make it out of this place alive, he couldn't miss a single shot. Alice was quick to hug him. Through tears she thanked him. But their moment of gratitude was short-lived as Katherine interrupted them.

"Guys, we ain't in the clear yet!"

The Silent Ones were approaching from both entrances

of the stairwells, and they were closing in quickly. Alice set Katherine up so she, too, could assist Miles in clearing their path to safety. Katherine put the rifle to her shoulder, looked down the scope, and shot at another one.

Body after body dropped, causing the others to trip and fall over one another. Miles didn't know how many more were coming. He didn't even know if they had enough ammo to take down the rest of them. All he knew was that they needed to escape. After he and Katherine took down a few more, he saw the opening they needed. Now was their chance.

Miles and Alice quickly grabbed Katherine and hoisted her up. They raced down the hall and past the laboratory as fast as they could, hoping no more monsters would appear in their pathway. It was the same path Dr. Tae-hyung had taken. As they approached the fire exit, one emerged from the open doorway, almost grabbing ahold of Miles and taking a bite out of his forearm. He pushed the monster off and put a bullet in its head. Then he released his hold on Katherine and used all of his body weight to shove the monster back down the steps. It collided with the mass of undead creeping up the stairwell, knocking them down like bowling pins.

"We gotta go!" Alice shouted, pulling at Miles's shirt.

Miles grabbed ahold of Katherine again and headed for the roof. The Silent Ones continued their sluggish pursuit as the three of them climbed the stairs. But when they arrived at the door, it was locked.

Miles jiggled the handle, but the door didn't move. "Fuck!"

He slammed his shoulder against it, trying to force it open. But again it didn't budge. He peered back at the monsters creeping toward them and let off a few more rounds until the clip was empty. They were seconds away from death. It seemed like all of their efforts were for nothing; the fuel Katherine used flying them to California, the time Beck and the others at the compound had spent treating his shoulder and feeding him, even the death of his parents. He'd managed to save his one true love from dying of a virus the North Korean government had created, but it wouldn't matter if he couldn't save her from getting her face mutilated.

But then an idea came to him.

Miles turned to Alice. "Let me see the gun."

She stopped shooting for a second to look at him. "What?! Why?"

"Quick! Hand me the gun!"

Alice threw him the gun. He used the butt of it to smash the door handle, but it didn't budge.

"They're comin'!" Katherine shouted.

Alice pulled Katherine to the side, pressing her back up against the door as Miles tried again. He hit the door over and over until the knob broke, freeing the lock and allowing them safe passage onto the roof.

When the door sprung open, Alice fell back onto the graveled roof, bringing Katherine down with her. Miles stepped toward them, but one of the undead caught him by the leg and took a chunk out of his calf. "AGHHH!!!"

"NO!!!" Alice screamed.

Miles had been bit. He knew that his chances of survival were nonexistent now that the person who had helped save Alice had disappeared. So he did what he thought he should do. He gazed deep into Alice's hazel eyes and accepted that their time together had come to an end.

With tears, he said, "I love you." Then suddenly—his hand pulling back on the door to close it—he turned and leaped into the horde, knocking them as far down the stairs as he could, allowing Alice and Katherine the chance to escape.

Alice was stunned. The love of her life—the boy who had given everything to help save her—was now gone.

As Alice tried to gather her composure, Katherine looked around in search of something to secure the door with. "There's nothin' up here to use as a prop. We gotta use our bodies."

Alice didn't say a word. Couldn't. She was still in shock. It was etched on her face.

"Alice, we need to do somethin'. C'mon."

Leaning to her good side, Katherine wrapped her arm around Alice and pulled her toward the door. A minute later, they had their backs pressed against the steel, listening to the humming footsteps of the Silent Ones piling up on the other side.

Miles tried his best not to cry out as the undead tore his body limb from limb, ripping the flesh from his bones and turning him into one of their own. But he now knew what it meant to be strong. To not give up. To be somebody. To truly live. He had come to the understanding that living in fear isn't really living whatsoever. Offering himself up to present a second chance at life to someone else—to someone he loved dearly—was the ultimate sacrifice. One that would never be forgotten.

As Alice and Katherine shared a moment of solace, catching their breaths with every inhale, they watched the helicopter in the distance disappear into the cloudy blue sky.

They were still alive thanks to Miles. He had done it. He had saved Alice. Saved them both. But they weren't in the clear yet.

29

The sun was high in the sky. They had no clue what to do next. There was no way to tell if the Skyhawk was salvageable from where they sat, their backs pressed against the door to prevent the undead from making it onto the roof. Even if the plane were salvageable, they realized, neither of them were in any condition to repair the vessel. Their chances of survival were diminishing by the second. Despite Miles's efforts, their risk of dying was higher than ever, given the swarm of the undead on the other side of the door.

"We could take a military vehicle," Alice said, whispering to keep as quiet as possible.

"Got the same issue as the plane, Alice," Katherine said. "Where we gon' get the fuel?"

They were in a predicament. Even if they found a vehicle full to the brim, they certainly couldn't make it back to Seattle on one tank of fuel. How on earth would they make it all the way to Seattle with no fuel?

The question gave Alice an idea.

"This is a naval base, right?" she asked.

Katherine wiped the sweat from her forehead. "Yeah."

Alice lifted her head and peered out at the airfield. Then she focused her eyes further west toward the coast, beyond the thin line of trees at the far end of the tarmac. There she caught a glimpse of what she'd been hoping to see: the tops of multiple masts moving in the wind. Back and forth they went, bobbing in the water.

Alice turned back to Katherine and pointed toward the coastline. "What doesn't require as much fuel, if any at all?"

Katherine's eyes widened. "A boat!"

"And not just any boat. A sailboat." From there it was agreed. They'd sail back home. "How's your hip?"

Katherine shifted her weight, wincing at the pain. "I can only handle so much pain, hon." She reached for Alice's hand. "I can't walk."

"Then you stay here." Alice patted Katherine's thigh, then grabbed the Winchester and moved to the ledge of the building, being careful not to make any noise. She laid on her stomach and looked through the sight, scoping out a route to the docks. There were only a few Silent Ones in their path. Five to be exact.

"I guess the rest are inside," she muttered. She aimed at one and pulled the trigger, but nothing happened. "Dammit. Out of ammo."

Alice peered back at Katherine and motioned to the empty clip in her hand. Katherine nodded back as she mouthed the words, *There's no more.*

Alice sighed as she stood and returned to the door alongside Katherine. "What now?"

Katherine reached into the inside pocket of her flannel and pulled out a tiny metal flask. "Miles worked his skinny little butt off to get us here. We'd better go down fightin'. I say let's get a move on."

She unscrewed the cap from the flask and downed the last of her liquor, attempting to numb her pain. She winced at the burning sensation in her throat as it went down.

Alice nodded. "Okay."

Standing, she wrapped Katherine's arm around her, then lifted. There was no telling what would happen once they left the door unattended. Alice didn't want to think about it. She didn't look back as she dragged Katherine across the roof to the ledge where a fire escape ladder stretched down to the ground below.

Alice helped Katherine onto the ladder first, then she followed. They both descended slowly to conserve as much energy as possible. Once Alice stepped foot on the asphalt, she dropped to one knee to help Katherine regain her balance. From there they trudged across the tarmac, Alice's eyes darting left and right in search of the undead. They had no ammo. No protection. Remaining quiet was of the utmost importance. Alice knew they had to be quick in securing a boat, but at the same time, it would be wise to take some time to look for a vessel that not only would be sufficient in getting them back home but also be stocked with enough provisions to help them survive the numerous days at sea.

The docks were only a couple hundred yards out; not too far from the runway. But there were still five Silent Ones in their midst. Huffing and puffing, they tried their best to slide past them, but it was of no use. They were too slow. The undead pursued them all the way to the gangway. All the boats rocked back and forth—from starboard to port—as the breeze trailed along the waterline. Every shift of the wind sent ripples in multiple directions.

Alice watched in fear as the undead staggered toward them. She turned and reached for the handle of the gate and pulled, the metal hinges squeaking as it opened. "Thank God, it's unlocked."

They passed through and stepped onto the floating walkway, then quickly closed the gate behind them. The two Silent Ones closest on their heels reached in between the bars for Katherine's body, their mouths gaping with blood drool. Katherine's shirt barely slipped from their grasps.

There was no telling how long the gate would hold, so Alice had to find a boat as quickly as possible. She immediately sat Katherine on the ledge of the dock and took off on her search. Every sailing vessel she passed looked too small for both of them. A few cabin cruiser motor yachts looked plenty big, but they would only leave them vulnerable to the dangers of the sea once they ran out of fuel. It had to be a sailboat—one that could withstand a coastal storm if they were to encounter one, God forbid.

The floating wooden dock creaked under Alice's feet as she continued her search for a proper vessel. When she finally found one that looked promising, she glanced back at Katherine to make sure the undead hadn't broken through the gate before boarding the vessel. She stepped into the cockpit and disappeared down the companionway. She sifted through every drawer and cupboard, turning up canned goods and two fishing rods. As long as the boat had enough propane, they'd be able to survive their days at sea.

We're going home, Miles! We're going to be okay!

But when Alice climbed back up the companionway and looked down the dock toward Katherine, she found the undead had broken through the gate. "Oh, no!"

Alice leaped from the boat to the dock and sprinted toward her friend. Katherine used her gun as a cane to stand, but it seemed to be no use. The Silent Ones were closing in on her. Alice managed to snatch her up just in time, dragging her down the dock until she reached the boat. The monsters were only a few feet away. In a panic, she pushed Katherine into the cockpit and used the rifle as a baseball bat. With all her might, she swung, knocking one monster into another and sending them both plummeting into the water.

Splash!

Then she swung again, catching the third one in the skull, but not after getting the butt of the rifle stuck in its head. It was set to join the others in the water below the docks, dragging Alice along with it, but at the last second, she released her grasp, losing the gun entirely. She watched as the woman slipped off the dock and crashed into the water, taking with her the only weapon she and Katherine had left to defend themselves with.

She exhaled. "That was close."

She was weaponless, but she was alive. There were no more monsters on the docks. If she could get the boat to sea before any more arrived, they would have no need for weapons anyway. Alice turned to Katherine with a relieved smile, but when she looked at her friend, she found her sniffling and wiping away tears. "What's wrong?"

"You didn't have to do that. Come back for me," Katherine replied. "I'm just an old woman. And now I'm a broken old woman at that. I'm just so grateful."

"After all that you've done for us?" Alice helped Katherine down the companionway and onto a leather bench as she continued to cry. "I'd never leave you behind. Never. Now, let's get outta here."

Alice started to step away, then froze. She'd been in a sailboat before, but she'd never sailed one single-handed. Wiping the tears from her cheeks, Katherine pointed at the chart table. "Look in there, hopefully, there's a manual inside. It should tell you everything you need to know."

Alice approached the teak chart table and opened the lid. There was nothing but junk inside, or at least what she thought was junk. She sifted through the clutter until finally she found the manual. The front cover read 2003 C&C 121. She skimmed the glossary, then flipped to the designated page. There she found information on the engine and its controls.

Alice traveled back up the companionway and into the

cockpit, then started the boat. The initial beep the diesel ignition let off, startled her. "Shit."

The sound was ear-piercing. She thought it would end, but it didn't. She didn't know how to shut it off, and she began to panic, knowing that if the sound persisted, it would lead all the undead within earshot directly toward the boat. She quickly pushed the start button, bringing the motor to life, and the sound ceased. Alice's heartbeat began to return to normal as she pushed the lever to increase the throttle until the boat started to move. Then it picked up in speed. They were on their way until—

The boat came to a halt. The motion was so jarring Alice almost got thrown from the cockpit into the water behind the transom. Looking back, she found that the vessel had been tied to two large cleats on the dock. Quickly reversing the throttle and backing the boat closer to the dock, she untied the ropes.

"What the hell's goin' on up there?" Katherine shouted from inside the boat.

"I gotta untie the boat from the dock so we can leave!" Alice shouted back.

Crack!

Her eyes darted to the gangway to find that two more monsters had ventured onto the dock, knocking the metal gate as such so it slammed closed. She quickly untied the second rope and jumped back onto the boat, nearly missing it in her rush. Determined to prevent the undead from getting onto the boat, Alice floored the throttle and turned the helm sharply. The slip they were in was fairly small for their 40-foot cruiser. The boat's fenders stood no chance as it scraped along the hull of the neighboring yacht; its flattened rubber tubes would be of no use going forward.

After a couple more close calls with other parked vessels and the surrounding concrete barriers that made up a majority of the marina, they finally made it out into San Francisco Bay, then further, into the Pacific Ocean. The breeze felt cool against Alice's skin, but it brought a calmness to her soul. Now she and Katherine could finally relax. They'd walked into a vicious trap, got what they wanted, and—mostly—made it out alive. They had succeeded. They were finally free.

I hope we reach Seattle soon. I couldn't think of anywhere else to go. Our provisions are running pretty low. Well, there wasn't really much, to begin with, but at least we had something. I haven't been so lucky at fishing. I've caught two in total, that's it. It's a shame, but hey, it's something. It's been one week now since we left Alameda, I think. I've lost track really. I feel like we wasted a lot of time, in the beginning, trying to understand the basics of sailing single-handed. Tacking and reefing the sails was an interesting ordeal. Regardless, I'm just glad whoever's boat we took had enough reading material onboard for us to go off of. Because if we didn't have this stuff we sure as hell would've had a tough time getting back.

I never knew how cold it could get out on the water. God, is it freezing out here. Especially at night. I know it's winter and all, but damn. There isn't enough huddling in the world that can keep us warm at night. Maybe if Miles were here, he could help keep us warm, but he isn't. I wish he was though. He could witness these sunsets. They're so beautiful. God, do I miss him. Hopefully, we won't be out here much longer. The chart-plotter shows that we're only a few miles from home now. I hope Serenity allows me back in. I hope she allows Katherine in, too.

Since I'm practically the only person who has survived a bite, I don't know if they'll be happy to see me, let alone believe that I'm me. They might think I'm some hybrid zombie or a twin or something. I don't know, really. All I know is that I hope they'll let us back in. There's so much I miss about that place. What I miss most, though, is the potato soup. I haven't been able to stop thinking about it since we left California. That's really the only thing I can remember from the compound right now. It's probably 'cause I'm so hungry. I think it's because the virus affected my appetite. I'm just so hungry now. More than ever. Or maybe it could just be 'cause I haven't eaten much lately. But all I know is that I can't wait to get home. And to see Sgt. Peppers. Oh, my sweet baby. I can't wait to see him.

Sincerely, A.W.

P.S. At the time I'm writing this, I think I can see the Space Needle. Maybe I should see if I can reach Boyd on the radio. God, I hope so.

Love this book?

Tell Markus.

Leave a review on...

www.amazon.com
www.goodreads.com